# PRAISE FOR PREVIOUS NOVELS

*The Natashas*

'A brave, original work . . . Moskovich's prose radiates with heat . . . written in a Cubist jumble of voices, languages, and textures, *The Natashas* reads as if one were spinning a radio dial of the world . . . [it] urges the reader to sink back in, connect, breathe'

Lauren Elkin, *Financial Times*

'Closest in tone and plot to a David Lynch film . . . confounding and beguiling in equal measure; prose that reads as heady yet ephemeral as smoke'

Lucy Scholes, *Independent*

'A haunting, unknowable novel, and no less beguiling for that'

*Daily Telegraph*

'A surreal and distinctively written exploration of identity . . . wonderfully original'

*Guardian*

'A hallucinatory torrent of imagery and ideas that moves entirely according to its own rules'

*Herald Scotland*

'A surreal, unknowable novel, reminiscent of a David Lynch film'

*Irish Times*

*Virtuoso*
## LONGLISTED FOR THE DYLAN THOMAS PRIZE 2020

'A bold feminist novel: it contains a world of love and friendship between women in which men and boys are both indistinct and irrelevant . . . *The Natashas* was a fascinating debut, *Virtuoso* is even better . . . a fully realized vision of a strange world'

*Times Literary Supplement*

'A hint of Lynch, a touch of Ferrante, the cruel absurdity of Antonin Artaud, the fierce candour of Anaïs Nin, the stylish languor of a Lana del Rey song . . . Moskovich's writing is compulsive and determined in its efforts to get at desire, grief and love'

*Guardian*

'Strikingly original . . . *Virtuoso* is a fine, fraught, strange novel'

*Observer*

'*Virtuoso* is powerfully mysterious and deeply insightful, a page-turner . . . a stirring endorsement of transgression on all fronts'

*LA Review of Books*

*A Door Behind a Door*

'We don't often see writing like this: genuinely subversive and innovative, an experiment in form that is actually discomfiting'

*Guardian*

'Part thriller and part narrative experiment, *A Door Behind a Door* is utterly unique'

*Buzzfeed*

'[A] sexy fever dream of a book, so visceral and poetic . . . Those who enjoy experimental forms, thought-provoking material, and a good thrill will delight in this haunting novel'

*LA Review of Books*

'A phantasmagoria about immigration, death, and queer desire with a plot that defies easy description . . . Moskovich has written a perplexing yet powerful work of literature that is likely to haunt the reader long after its last page'

*Chicago Review of Books*

'Moskovich draws on Clarice Lispector, Sophie Calle, and even Pauline Réage, as she moves around the page, the body, the world'

*BOMB Magazine*

# Nadezhda in the Dark

# Nadezhda in the Dark

## Yelena Moskovich

FOOTNOTE

First published in 2023 by
Footnote Press

www.footnotepress.com

Footnote Press Limited
4th Floor, Victoria House, Bloomsbury Square, London WC1B 4DA

Distributed by Bonnier Books UK, a division of Bonnier Books
Sveavägen 56, Stockholm, Sweden

First printing
1 3 5 7 9 10 8 6 4 2

A CIP catalogue record for this book is available from the British Library

ISBN (hardback): 978-1-804-44048-3
ISBN (ebook): 978-1-804-44049-0

Printed and bound in Great Britain
by Clays Ltd, Elcograf S.p.A.

*И вот одна я в комнате моей.*
*Опять одна, а это значит – с Вами.*

*And so, alone, in this room of mine,*
*Alone again, which means – with you.*

– Irina Kant

Nadezhda, her hair hangs like milk,
like thick, dark milk,
her face in profile, her forehead crescent,

there's the tip of her nose
sticking out from the thickness of her milky hair,
on the darkest hour of the darkest day of a Berlin black-milk winter,
    the trees
crack in the wind, the puddles
catch the black sky, trickle it downstream along the curb and slick
    the bars of the iron gutter with it,

I don't mean to slyly conjure up a prison,
as if
to imply
that Nadya and I live in a prison,
Nadya and I do not live in a prison,
we are free,
we know people who live in a prison,
people our age who have lived in a prison,
and go on living in a prison, they are not
free,

people younger than us and older than us,
and people not yet born in the bellies of people who live in a prison,
    and of course
everyone's grandparents and great-grandparents
spent some time in labour camps,
they were not like us —
free,

1

the wind blows
from the passing train of the Neukölln U-Bahn station a couple of
    streets down,
from the wide-open field that was once the Tempelhof airport,
from the end of the day,
from the beginning of the night,
from the blackness that's thickening in the north,
of the Baltic Sea,
from our friend Pasha leaving footprints in the snow,
from the sons of poetesses,
from the stiff old Kharkov to shattered new Kharkiv
and from Moscow
raided of its youth,
to the south-east of Berlin,
sweeping down Ilsestraße,
gusting upward to the fifth floor,
into the open window of our living room,
across the fog-grey couch and the round silver table and the vacuumed
    beechwood floor
through the door ajar
to our milk-dark bedroom,
into the nostrils of Nadya
sitting on the edge of the bed,
and out of my mouth,
sitting beside her
in the dark,

we are here
in our bedroom
sitting knee to knee,

I'm in my double-XL men's black sweater,
the cable knit fraying, bunched sleeves
at the wrist, and the loose navy-blue Adidas sweatpants,
I cinched up the drawstring so they stay on my hips,
I also rolled them over, they fit best that way, Nadyenka
is still wearing her outdoor clothes, normally
she doesn't sit on the bed in her outdoor clothes,
her black jeans that she's been wearing every day, they pinch
her belly, but she says she's going to lose weight soon, she doesn't want

to get a size up, they look
uncomfortable, the stiff denim pulls and wavers around the zipper,
    she says
they're comfortable,
she still has her black blazer on, the one she wore to work at the
    salon today, the one she's been wearing to work every day at the
    salon, and for the private
clients, it has wide boxy shoulders
and sits lax on her frame, and the black men's tee
underneath, tucked in, and her sterling-silver chain with the heart
    charm
hanging in the crux
of her throat, I don't
look good in necklaces, I've tried
all kinds, Nadya agrees, she's never met anyone
who doesn't look good in necklaces, but I have
a sterling-silver necklace with a charm heart that hangs
in the crux
of my throat too, we both do,
it's the only necklace that looks good on me, Nadyenka hasn't changed
her clothes, I've been
home all day so I haven't changed mine
either, we are both
quiet,

we can hear the trains,
the exit
where the junkies shoot up,
past the building that's been under scaffolding
for years now,

around the corner from our grainy building on Ilsestraße,
in the daylight,
the Kurdish kids drive their plastic trucks in the cracks of the
    sidewalk year round,
and everyone steps over them,
and that's their playground,
but at night there's no one,
'cause the streetlights don't work on that side of the street
where the Kurdish kids play

and listen to the trains
come and go
as their plastic trucks go
rrrum rrrum,
and those streetlights haven't worked for years now,
and so the junkies go there
to light up where there is no light,
with their wiry hair
and puckered jaws,
'cause they say Neukölln is not safe,

even in the daytime, Nadyenka says, Please,
let's not kiss and such
here,
it's not safe,

it is dark here on Ilsestraße, fifth floor, in the darkest
hour of the darkest
day of a Berlin black-milk winter, and we have chosen
not to turn on the light,

You need darkness
to be loved, that's something
Pasha would say,
he's still here, he sleeps in
stanzas, he sleeps
like a kitten, his wrists crossed and tucked
under his chin, there is a stanza
with insomnia, it climbs through my thoughts,
there is a stanza
by Sophia Parnok,
our Russian Sappho, it climbs
up the stairs,

there is a stanza
about yesterdays and tomorrows
being swept away,
she's one of the Xerox saints
of the Russian-speaking dykes and faggots,
and Pasha had used up his pocket change

on making copies
of verses
that were keeping him alive,
he knew them like the back of his hand,
he wasn't the only faggot
to know the backs of hands,
anyways, it took him seconds
to commit them to memory, he had one of those
brains the KGB could have used,
he recited Parnok and other poetesses and poets,
mostly poetesses,
mothers, mothers,
and it was always too heartfelt, we should have known,
it was winter then,
it's always winter,
and it is winter now,
the window was open then,
the window is always open,
the window is open now,
Pasha,
then, always, now,
yesterdays and tomorrows,
he had his shirt off,
he finished the poem,
he put his shirt back on,

I'm in therapy and Nadezhda is not,

though she was for a year after she opened her mailbox and
    received the police report,
that was long ago now,
she said she's got no more tears for that,
she's over it,

I've got too many tears,
it's part of my diagnosis,

the balcony
of our apartment here on Ilsestraße, fifth floor,
is a sort of red-stone enclave,

it has a black metal railing and half-empty flower containers
we haven't taken in, the soil that's left is frozen,
somewhere in there are the seeds that were trying to be flowers,
those who made it
were bushy yellow Santolinas
and dwarf spruces (because they reminded Nadyenka of Moscow)
and lavender for its scent and loyalty,

here in this Berlin black-milk winter,
on Ilsestraße, fifth floor,
there are no more flowers
in the half-empty containers
clipped onto the icy black metal railing,

if I turn my head away from Nadyenka,
I can see the red-stone balcony through the open door,
but I don't need to turn my head to see
the red-stone balcony
like my babushka Anya's artificial artery,

I don't need to turn my head to see
the past,

the surgeon who inserted that artery into babushka Anya was a big
    reader, he said
he loved Russian literature, what great literature,
there's no one like Gogol,
and there is no one
like my babushka,
the surgery went well, *Baruch Hashem,*
she recovered at the hospital in Tzfat, in the north of Israel, then
    my dedushka took her home to the village in the mountains
    called Ibikur, made up of old Soviet women and men,
Ukrainian and Russian and Belorussian women and men,
in this village everyone spoke Russian,
a Soviet valley
in the desert
of a desert country
where my grandfather and grandmother and great-grandmother
    emigrated from Soviet Ukraine and then died,
one by one,

back then in Ibicur we had Vova,
who also emigrated from old Kharkov with his wife and his son
and his son met an Israeli girl
and they had a son too, I don't remember his name,
Vova had a car,
a four-door white Mazda, he was proud
of it and all the old folks of Ibicur were proud
of it too, 'cause he gave them a lift when they needed a lift,
when my prababushka Gala (my babushka Anya's mama)
died, he drove my grandparents to the cemetery at the bottom of
    the valley,
next to the army training base,
so they could wash her tombstone
and put plastic flowers at the foot of her grave,

the doctors inserted that artery
so that babushka Anya could live two more years,
she lived four more years, *Baruch Hashem*,
then died a week before her birthday,

Mamachka and I flew in for the funeral,
her from America, me from France,
and Vova drove us all down, in his four-door white Mazda, into
    the valley,
next to the army training base,
and we washed the tombstones of my babushka Anya and my
    prababushka Gala
and put plastic flowers at the foot of their graves,

Mamachka told me that sick people always
die just before their birthday,

my dedushka Itzhak (the Jewish name he took when he immigrated,
he was the only one who believed in the whole thing,
the Torah and the heat and being loved by the desert)
he died
ten days before his birthday,
and my mamachka and papachka flew over from America
for his funeral (I stayed in France,
I had my reasons), Vova drove

7

them all down, in his four-door white Mazda, into the valley, next
    to the army training base,
and they washed all three tombstones
and put plastic flowers at the foot of each grave,

my dedushka died ten days before his birthday,
eight months after my babushka died
a week before her birthday,
and then my birthday was approaching
and I wanted to die
for no good reason
on a free continent
in a country
with no war,

I was not right in the head
I guess,
or terrified that
I was not right in the head,

I tried to keep writing
and chasing tail
and then hiding from it,
saying no one could love me,
and cowering at my mother's voice on the phone asking me
why don't I find a man – or, all right, a woman,
a good woman to take care of you,
Mamachka, I'm a war-child
with no war,
I didn't know how to explain it to her,
who would have guessed that I'd live long enough to meet someone
like Nadya,

then it was summer and then it was autumn
and my mama got endometrial cancer
and then it was winter,
the slowest winter
of her life,
counting down the days to her birthday

in February
and then the day came
when she had been born
and here she was
not dead,

I was still angry an ocean away,
I was back to hating myself instead of sleeping
in the nest I made
when I ran away to Paris –
forgive the cliché,
but I did,
simply because if I was going to die somewhere
it wouldn't be in America,
but really I didn't want to die,
I wanted to live, God,
I loved life,

who the hell knows how many years I spent
sitting in a routine stupor on the floor
of my tiny one-room flat
on rue Dolomieu,
that I could barely afford,
indignant with my own self for barely affording shit,
for my life that I could barely sustain,
for my writing that was the only thing keeping me alive,
but wasn't giving me anything to live off,

despite the demons in my head
(that would later be diagnosed)
I kept choosing beauty,
and that's got to count for something,

they say Ukrainians are brave,

I squeezed every ounce of my Ukrainian blood and said to myself,
God, you love life,
and don't you off another Ukrainian Jew
(it was a dark sort of joke and dark sorts of jokes kept me going),

to be honest, I don't like nationalistic bravery,
I don't like how heroism feels,

brave people are brave,

I've stood on the edge of such insignificant downfall,

after crying so hard and so long that I vomited,
I sat on my well-worn futon and recited a poem whose beauty
made me want to stay in this world,

one like the one
by Brodsky, you know,
the one about staring out the window at an aspen,
the one about loving deeply but not often,

I can feel when Nadyenka smiles even when my back is to her,
I can feel when she opens her mouth and parts her lips and shows
    the edge of those balletic teeth
even in the dark,
the top row, firm, side by side,
and the bottom overlap here and there like a folk dance,
and I love her mouth,
I love her teeth,
I love her,

you can only live inside a stanza for so long,

I still tear myself up for those years I was
thinking without thinking
about being without being
and walking without walking
into traffic,

(I didn't do it, to my therapist's relief,
the decision left me indifferent
for days,
and then suddenly
it scared me for a thousand years),

I continued to have episodes,
seduced by the speeding wheels of a Citroën,


in this Berlin black-milk winter,
on Ilsestraße, fifth floor,
the wind blows up from the street
and Nadya shifts her knee
then places it back,

three years ago,
when my mama almost died,
the days of February fell like O. Henry's leaves
(you know that one story he wrote
where there's this young woman who moves from a rural town to
    the Big Apple,
she wants to be a painter,
and she meets another young woman at a restaurant on Eighth Street,
and she wants to be a painter too,
they decide to move in together
where the outcasts who dream
of a world
yet to come
live together,
the rent is cheap,
even if the apartments are dirty,
Greenwich Village it is,
at least
they are free,

they feel graced
with a purpose,
the first young woman says this is only the beginning,
one day
she wants to go to Italy
and paint the Bay of Naples,
her roommate says, I'm sure you will,
they are kind

to each other,
because they mother
each other's
dreams, the first young woman's room has one window,
one small window, she likes to keep it open
for the fresh air
and to waft out the smells of the paints,
a wind blows up
from the street through her window,
her small open window,
it blows up and they say it's no good,
it's real bad,
It's pneumonia, the doctor says
to the first young woman,
her paints and brushes and easel
sit in the corner
as she coughs and coughs and coughs
in her damp, sweat-stained sheets,
her roommate brings her cheap broth
and tells her it will pass,
soon enough she'll be
in the Bay of Naples,
the sick young woman
can't laugh,
it hurts her ribs,
her roommate closes the small curtain
of her small window,
and tells her to sleep,
the sick young woman closes her eyes
and sees a bay
full of black-milk water
ebbing towards her toes,
the doctor tells her roommate
in the hallway
the chances are slim,
pneumonia is cruel,
the winds grow icy and forceful
there is a big tree
between her building and the red-brick one across the way,
she can see it outside her small window,

she tells her roommate to keep the curtain open,
she can't sleep anyways,
she stares at the branches, and the leaves on those branches,
dark green and yellow,
curl and dry and fall off,
she dreams of the black-milk waters,
she tells her roommate that when the last leaf falls
she will die,
her roommate begs her,
it's nonsense, together
they share a dream,
the roommate sets up her easel and canvas and paints
in the room with the small window
to keep her sick best friend,
her only friend in the big, cold city,
company,
I will paint while you sleep,
you shouldn't have to be alone,
but all those who close their eyes
are alone,
the roommate goes downstairs
to get the old painter on the floor below,
he's in his forties, but he's been scrunched up
by life,
a drunk but has a good face
to paint, lots of creases and shadows,
and something in his eyes, despite it all,
everyone in the building has heard it,
he says one day he'll paint a masterpiece,
he's been saying that for two decades,
he paints shit and he drinks,
and he sits for other painters
who like to paint his face
and he collects small change from it
that he uses to buy more booze,
he comes up and takes a seat
in front of the easel,
You look awful
he tells the bedridden woman,
Well, she says,

I'm going to die,
all three look out the small window,
there is only one leaf,
dark green and yellow,
barely clinging
on the last fibres
of its stem
it's a cold New York winter,
some say
the coldest New York winter
in all the cold New York winters,
that leaf stands
no chance,
tomorrow morning, the young woman thinks,
I will be dead,
her roommate has done her work for the day,
she gives the old man some change
and tells him to come back tomorrow,
she goes to close the curtain
of the small window, Please,
the sick young woman says,
keep it open,
and the black-milk night
comes into her room,

the next morning,
the New York City streets are feathery white, the air
is sharp and polar, the girl's eyes
flutter open and her gaze drifts to the window, where, to her surprise,
the leaf
is still there,
dark green and yellow,
holding tight
to its branch,
she feels different, everything
is going to be different,
she gets up and calls her roommate,
both women squeeze their faces
into the small window
and stare at the brave little leaf,

her roommate tells her to stay in bed and puts her paints away, the
    old man
is a no-show,
probably drunk somewhere,
the days go by, the sick young woman
is less and less sick,
she eats, she gets out of bed, she even
picks up her paintbrush and draws waves
into the air,
the doctor visits, he says she's a lucky girl,
pneumonia is cruel,
it took someone a couple of nights ago,
an old man who lived downstairs,
the young women inquire,
The painter,
the old painter?
I suppose, the doctor says,
he was a painter, though not
a very good one, he chuckles,
when the doctor leaves, the young women
rush to the small window,
they stare at that curious little leaf,
the wind blows and blows,
but the leaf
does not move,
not even a shutter,
not even a wince,
the young women bundle up and head downstairs
into the alley
covered with snow,
where the tree grows,
they look up and stare
at the stiff little leaf,
a painted leaf,
so life-like
that it gave life
back to the sick young woman,
at their feet
smudges of dark green and yellow paint,
they hurry up the stairs, the old man's door is open,

He had nobody, the neighbours say, Take what you want,
the place is a mess, his old shoes
splattered with paint,
dark green and yellow,
the young women take
nothing,
they return to their apartment and part ways,
the first young woman goes to the small window
and beholds the masterpiece),

my mama loved that story
so much,
she mentioned it many times at the kitchen table
with a teary eye
(for a woman who otherwise believed crying leads to high cholesterol
    and premature dementia),
and she rehashed other O. Henry stories,
because he always wrote these tragic stories,
and all of his stories were translated into Russian –
we had more translated works published
than our own work
in our own language
(I mean the Russian language, 'cause back then the Ukrainian
    language was considered a rural tongue) –
there was a snow storm
on my mama's birthday too,
and she didn't die after her surgery
or chemo or radiation
and we celebrated her birthday without her uterus,

here, the snow has melted,
it's cold but not
cold enough,
Nadya and I are sitting
knee to knee,
in our bedroom,
on Ilsestraße, fifth floor,

Nadya's thighs lean towards each other,
she lifts her forearms and lays her hands palm up on her lap,

so that they are open to the dark,
she often keeps them that way, as if trying
to let go of something,
is it too simple if I say
it's something like a bird, that's it's a bird, that
she's trying to let go of a bird,
but the bird
has already flown away?
Nadyenka,

in the dark,
Nadya likes to turn on the flashlight on her phone and go
to the small window in our bedroom and flash it at the rooftop
of the building across the street
and click her tongue calling the cats,
and the cats from the building across the street come out onto the
    rooftop,
and we see two green pearls of their eyes look our way,
and we point and meow at them with stretched nasal voices,
it's silly and exhilarating, we could spend whole evenings
chasing the roof cats with her phone
in the dark,

it's not cold enough
for the snow to stick,
but it's too cold for the cats to come out on the roof,
so we are just sitting
in the dark,

when you meet the right person
they give you back the years of your life
that you thought you had wasted,

it's been over a year since I've considered stepping off
the light of this world
into my own grave,

knee to knee,
she is quiet,
we are both quiet,

Nadya's told me so much about herself,
about her ex-wife
and her years in Moscow,
she's told me
about dreams
she had, and that they warned her,
and that she hadn't listened
until it was too late,

Nadya's a resilient person,
but has cycles of regret that take getting used to,

I don't know what's she thinking,

knee to knee, I'm sitting
next to Nadya, my Nadezhda,
her given name, which means 'hope' in Russian,
how could you name a child Hope
and tell her she's worthless?

Soviet mothers,
their hope was choked out of them
by their Soviet mothers
and their Soviet motherland,
my Nadya, my Nadezhda,
how did you manage to keep your name alive?
my Nadya, my Nadezhda, my Hope
is sitting
on the edge
of the bed, her back
curves in and her shoulders settle
low and soft, my hands
roll on my thighs and close into each other,
my hands tend
to close into each other,
I'm one of those people
who sit down and lace
their fingers together and lay
that clump on their thighs,

we're both sitting
with our hands in our laps,
each in our own way,

Nadya told me
weeks ago
that she dreamed of her ex-wife's cat,
Dasik
(an Armenian name, because Armenians have the most beautiful
    names),
a Scottish Fold with a round grey face, Dasik loved Nadya
more than her owner, the ex-wife,
more than her cat food,
more than chasing a house fly,
in Nadyenka's dream
Dasik looked at her with this sort of human stare, and then
his eyes just fell out of his head,

in this Berlin black-milk winter,
on Ilsestraße, fifth floor, the wind laces
from the open window,
we don't shiver,

in Yiddish there is a saying, and it goes like this:
*Mit a lefl ken men dem yam nit oys'shepn,*
You can't empty the ocean with a spoon,

I was hurt very young,
but, then again,
all Soviet children were hurt very young, we grew up
saying 'us' and 'we', it was the public Lenin's 'us'
and the private Yevgeny Zamyatin's *We,*
and still
we were,
and had always been,
alone, we had songs
about lovesickness,

and they were really cool,
and we couldn't wait to catch them on TV,
like Alla Pugacheva with her poofy red hair and her if-you-don't-
    like-it character,
when she performed 'Mne Nravitsya' (I like it . . . )
– it was Marina Tsvetaeva's poem put to song –
she sang it with her signature lip curl,
looking out into nowhere,
with that anti-hero zeitgeist of Tsvetaeva,
she likes it that
the person she loved
doesn't love her anymore
and she likes it that
she does not love the person
who loved her anymore,
and what a relief
to not love the one we used to love, Tsvetaeva
hung herself at age forty-eight, just over five weeks
before her birthday, not sure
if that's close enough
to hold up my mama's theory,

Nadyenka loves Alla Pugacheva and so do I,
I mean she was the shit
and had the attitude for it,
and she's still kicking twenty-five years
after Tsvetaeva (who was also the shit,
but in the wrong era),

Pugacheva tried to stay out of it,
the war in Ukraine and so on, and things happened,
and things happened, her youngest children
went to school in Moscow, her husband
got blacklisted as a foreign agent, and her kids got their share
at school, why their papachka's a traitor,
and Pugacheva knows how to throw a punch *v'mordu*
a good slug *blyad*, sometimes
it's a bit much even, but hey, she's a rock star,
and so she declared herself a foreign agent too, and put
her castle, yes, she owned a castle, in Moscow

up for sale,
and immigrated with her family to Israel,

Nadya and I made love
earlier today,
we ate each other out
simultaneously,
one of our favourite positions,
she came first (like she usually does in this position),
and then we flipped over and she fingered me deep
in a way I can only explain as
virtuosic,
no one has ever fingered me
like her,
she can make me come with those fingers,
all muscle and grace,
like Adam touching God,

we hadn't done it in a while actually, I had a lot of anxiety
and was taking medication for it, I had trouble
with my moods
and was taking medication for it, I had some real steep downs
and I was taking medication for it,
I was and am on a lot of medication, sometimes I'm fine,
good,
great even,
and then something will change, and the whole treatment
will derail, and I get messed up again,
and we change the milligrams of this or that
with my psychiatrist,
and talk about this and that
with my therapist,
and I spend half my days in bed
or in the half-filled bathtub
with a swollen face from all the crying, while Nadya
makes me stick out my tongue
and drips some sort of potion
her babushka used to take, when she was a living grouch,
to calm her nerves,
made of flower extracts and alcohol,

she brought over bottles from Moscow
just for me, they are the only thing that calm me down,
or get me a little drunk,
along with the medication
they put me to sleep, yes,
naked in the hollow tub
with my belly twisted
facing away from Nadya
I sobbed and pleaded with her
to just leave, it was a test,
I wanted to see if she would really abandon me, or to see how much
I could get away with,
or, as my therapist would say,
to just ask
for help
with whatever words I could,

everybody knows
Tolstoy and Dostoevsky and Chekhov, and if you're bookish
Bulgakov and Gogol and Pasternak,
but
who's talking about Margarita Khemlin
who died a handful of years back
and left us with a masterpiece,
*Klotsvog,*

sometimes at night, when Nadya has already fallen asleep next to
    me and the blinds on the slanted window of our bedroom are
    not fully shut, I lay on my back and
glimpse the broad night-time sky,
a dark milky sky,
a pauper's sky,
a dreamer's sky,
a prisoner's sky,
and I think about the sea
and sailors lying in their cot,
like me,
except alone,
looking up at a broad night-time sky,
a dark milky sky,

a doomed sky,
as they think about land,


I won't ruin the whole story,
but in the beginning, in *Klotsvog*, the main character, Maya,
– who's evacuated with her family from the little town of Ostyor in
    Ukraine when she's very little, where the then-thriving Jewish
    population is near erased – and, skip ahead, the past is the
    past,
she's trying to make it in the big city,
but, of course, she falls for the wrong type of guy
and has a baby too young,
a boy
named
Misha, she can't raise him
so she sends him to her parents (who are back in Ostyor),
and they take in the boy and raise him on Yiddish instead of
    Russian ('cause sometimes when you survive you fall in love with
    the language that almost killed you), some years later, Maya
    takes Misha back,
she's horrified that he has learned Yiddish, after all she has done
to rid the boy
of his Jewishness
(bribes and paperwork)
for his own good, dammit, doesn't he realise, after all that's hap-
    pened,
he's still little, he's so little,
he's afraid of the dark, she tells him,
Only speak Russian, he bumbles
words in Yiddish, even though she tells him
Only speak Russian, damnit, he blurts out Yiddish
even in public, she has no choice, she takes
to hard parenting, and, when he cries at night, in the dark,
she doesn't come
to him, unless he speaks Russian,
Only Russian, Misha,
there he is, all alone, all night, whimpering
in Yiddish
in the dark,

our mothers,
our Slavic mothers, our tough-love mamkas,
our beloved mothers, *mame ikh hab mura,*
*muter, muter,* Mama, I'm scared,
little by little, Misha learns,
years later,
Maya goes from one husband to another,
gets herself an apartment in Moscow
with a phone
(a luxury of the time),
and her new husband brings in the dough, she's wearing gold,
gold that Misha, a young man now,
asks how she can wear
gold
from the teeth of Jews, Misha
joins the navy, Maya's all alone in her big apartment
with her modern phone
and she picks it up
and listens to the dead tone,
then takes an inhale,
and starts speaking
to no one, Misha's far away with the navy
not because he's a patriot,
or a man's man, but to get the hell away
from his mama, he lies on his cot
and I'm not sure but I think he looks out
at the dark milky sky
like me,

Misha, my Mishenka,
a grown man now,
on a fleet in the Indian Ocean,
(how attached I get to the people I meet in novels, a Slavic tradition,
we cried more for fictional characters than those
sleeping next to us)

there is a moment, a rare moment,
when Maya is not running around,
shopping or smoothing things over,
in the blankness of one early morning she wakes up from a dream

where Misha didn't know how to swim, and he was
afraid,


Nadezhda is resilient,
I don't know what she's thinking,
but she could be wondering
if we might try and see, just see if by chance
a cat has braved
the cold
and snuck up on the roof,
though I know she knows,
as I know,
that it's too cold for the cats to come on the roof, Nadyenka and I,
we both remember what a piece of candy meant
in our youth,
the whole world stopped at the sweetness on the edges of a child's
    mouth,
Nadezhda is resilient,
but that doesn't mean it's enough to make it past thirty
with the will to live,


and that doesn't mean that we didn't love life,
God, I loved life, and I think Pasha did too,
even though he didn't always act like it, he read too much
Tsvetaeva and Akhmatova,
thought of himself like their son,
he had a ma and a pa, but it's not enough,
people like us,
delicate people, you know,
we need mothers in the form of verse,
God, we loved life, so why
did Pasha's heart go soft as a peach,
and slimed off at the slightest touch?
*Mame,*
*ikh hab mura,*


last weekend, the sun came out in Berlin
and Nadyenka and I decided to celebrate
the lightness of a light sky,

amongst other things,
things we'd rather not say we were celebrating,
like a lift in a bout of regret rolling off Nadya's tongue
about her ex-wife,
and the years of life she had lost,
not just any years
but her late twenties and early thirties, and Nadya kept
repeating herself, then saying it's all behind her,
and me, I didn't know what to say,
I hate the woman I don't know,
and I'm losing patience for the woman I love,
and then we find each other
like we always do, Go
to the darkest day of the darkest breath of your darkest word and
    I will
still find you,
Nadezhda,

it was a Saturday,
a sunny Saturday,
we sat outside on Karl-Marx-Straße,
me with my heavy leather jacket zipped up, black scarf wound,
a moto-dude silhouette with a 1920's face,
and her, a rose and caramel silk scarf wrapped around her head
    and her Masha eyes, as blue as a husky, in her big navy bomber
    zipped and puffed,
she's my Russian Bonnie,
I'm her Ukrainian Clyde, we can see our breath
as we drink our milky coffees,
and peck at the black and green olives,
and fork the cured meats with the sliced cucumbers and tomatoes,
and spread jam and honey on chunks we break off the sesame
    *simits*, and nibble at the pistachio pastry that I don't like, but I
    nibble anyways,
when you're in love
you'll nibble anything,
I clean my palette with the cheese and spinach *pirozhki* that she lets
    me have,
and we usually get a second milky coffee,
and have more honey, Nadya loves honey,

26

I watch her pour it all over her last piece of bread
and it drips and puddles on the white oval plate,

there's another Yiddish saying, and it goes like this:
*Men ken nit ariberloyfn di levone,*
You can't outrun the moon,

Raya, my mamachka's old friend who stayed in Kharkiv with her
    disabled husband, Borya, when everyone left,
when the Russians first invaded,
Raya and Borya didn't have any children who lived abroad, they
    didn't have any children period,
they had each other,
and Borya had his wheelchair,
so they stayed and listened
to the gunfire and bombs outside their window,
they used to have a cat, an orange kitty-cat, who passed a couple
    years back,
Raya and Borya loved cats, so my mamachka would send Raya
    videos of cats she found on the internet, where they did
unexpected, silly things, they had no electricity
last week, so Raya couldn't charge her phone, but this week it's back,
Raya loved the last video my mama sent,
a fuzzy grey kitten who takes a big running start and ends up
    sliding across the whole span of a linoleum kitchen floor with
    astonished galactic-blue eyes –
it's better seen than described,
I rewatched it many times,
it's a good one to rewatch, it's really, really
cute, this year Raya and Borya started lighting candles
for Shabbat, just in case
God sees
the two pearl tips of fire
in the rubble
of the earth,
last time,
none of the glass broke in their apartment, though
it broke in the apartment next door,
there was a rain of gunshots and this constant feeling
that the building was going to plummet,

Kolya in Bashtanka told my mama on a Zoom call
with a couple of other old classmates that the tanks just appeared
from the thick of the forest,
and Sashyenka
mentioned on that Zoom call
(after he got his mic to work)
that the building a couple of streets down was hit,
a family looked for their nephew,
or son-in-law,
no, nephew, he had just turned sixteen,
they couldn't find him, they looked and looked,
they finally got into the basement (there was
a lot of fallen wood to remove)
and there he was,
he had been lying there
for four days,
he was shot in the ear,
they buried him in the courtyard of the building,
Milachka,
who was looking great despite her escalating diabetes,
talked about her daughter in Germany, she's a dentist, my mama
mentioned that I'm in Germany too, Sashyenka
cracked a joke, Sashyenka
is so witty, Mama told me, he just has this
sense of humour
and perfect timing,
I think she still has a crush on him,
from their mathematics college days,

some people say
don't feel sad for the Russian boys,
what happened
to the sons of poetesses?

Bucha, Izyum, and Irpin, the shot kneecaps,
the stack of bodies on Yablunska Street
set on fire, thighs and stomachs
eaten away by the abandoned dogs, starved
and lost, cats meowling in apartments left locked

in the rush, the anonymous young woman
telling the journalist everything with a tongue
outrunning time, she's saying, Write it down, the translator is telling
    the man
with the pen, Write it down, there was a long queue
for the pharmacy, waiting for hours for heart medication,
insulin, inhaler refills, the line of people flinching,
some crouching, as dirt and concrete burst within eyesight, all those
    stanzas
of the poetry we share,
Konstantin Simonov's 'Wait for me',
the soldier ballad, our brotherly poem,
the newspaper *Pravda* printed it in 1942, soldiers
cut it out, memorised it, the torn piece found
in the breast pockets
of corpses, *Wait for me*
*and I'll come back, only*
*truly wait,*
soldiers on both sides still cantillate
the same verse,
Russian boys
sent off to the snow-glazed tundra
of nowhere, without proper equipment, no radio signals in the night,
faulty ammunition, no medical aid, stocking up
on boxes of tampons in villages
to stick in their bullet wounds, some
went to the border proudly, even
blood-thirsty, and some for parental dogma,
and some had the right person to bribe, and some were prisoners
    forced to,
and some tried to run, and some didn't want to die,
but shouted, Shoot, shoot
at the Ukrainian soldier
holding up his gun, some had served
in 2014, and, back then, some were haughty
pushing into southern Ukraine, and they are not so haughty
anymore, some are still haughty
because, if they gave it up,
it would be worse than death,

Nadya says she's gained too much weight,
but fuck it,
let's eat what we want to eat, if the world
is coming to an end, in secret,
I think I gained too much weight too, God knows,
we poke each other's bellies,
and laugh about it, if we want
we can lose it together, a couple of kilos
for me and I'd be happy, Nadya wants
to lose five to six kilos, maybe,
maybe we'll give it a try, in truth, I'm okay
with my extra kilos, I'd rather
just get baggier
clothes and coats
with broader shoulders,
look at Chernobyl, that was just one reactor, imagine
if several reactors blow, it'd reach North America, forget Berlin,
    who cares
if I've got an extra
kilo to spare,

we got the new
lease to stay here, on Ilsestraße, fifth floor,
the papers are sitting on the kitchen table,
under a big clouded stone
we brought back from Spain,

we have everything
in its place,
our box of dildos
below the bed
and, in the drawer near the door, my medication
and the journal of when I take what and how much,
to stay on top of things, 'cause, God,
I love life, and, God,
I love Nadyenka, and, I won't say where,
but well-hidden, our passports
and some money, in dollars and euros,
you never know, I'm right here,
Nadyenka said when she squeezed my damp,

cold shoulder in the hollow tub, my eyes
so slippery in my skull,

the pages of the calendar
on the wall in the kitchen
flutter with each gust of wind
from the open window,
we had bought it with great resolution,
but slid the unopened calendar between two books
and forgot about it, we pinned it up
only in September,
we had wasted
all those other months, and we were slow
to start using it, but by October we filled in doctor's appointments
     and dinners and our periods, December was hanging, today
was marked in blue pen with Nadya's hand, *Winter*,
it was the first day
of winter, Nadya marked the first days
of the seasons, as if nature
was benevolent
for those who followed her clock, last New Year's we were also
     here,
in Berlin, Pasha
joined us, Nadya
was not happy about it, she wanted me
all to herself, I was worried
about Pasha, with Nadya it was hard
to be worried about someone else, What if I got cancer,
Nadyenka had said, would you run off to Chicago
with Pasha? I told her I don't like
Chicago, but, goddammit, you're not
my owner, No, she said, but I'm your
Hope,

I don't want to fall in love
like a couple of runaways,
Nadya
popped open a bottle of champagne she got on a bulk deal,
the one Scarlett Johansson endorses,
it's just a standard French champagne, Moët,

nothing special, but that's how I know
I'm a snob, .
a Parisian, after over a decade and two passports,
or maybe it was always me, or maybe
being junk in the eyes of society
makes one hoard cultural prestige,
it was never the prestige of commodities
(which my kind is not party to), it was the prestige
of personal taste, and I considered mine
superior, I'm ashamed
to admit it, but I believe
taste is a talent (and myself as bestowed), how can a girl
give up her tight grip
on the sky? I too am the son
of poetesses,
I'm a bird,
the bird between Nadyenka's palms,
the bird that has long
gone, the bird that
is free
like us,

it was a special New Year's because I had come to understand
(through years of loving deeply and not often),
that I was actually devastating
my time on earth,

and I'm trying, I'm really trying
not to get high off
my neglected youth,
okay, I still
get a little high off
my neglected youth, we drank the champagne,
Nadya, Pasha, and I,
on the last day of an old year
and the first day of a new year, I was trying
to avoid alcohol, 'cause number one,
it's not great with my meds, and number two,
it really gets me down, that night we got drunk,
which is rare for us, Nadya also doesn't really drink, she did

coke for some years a long time ago, mainly in Moscow (where
    it's much cheaper – to those with Euro cash, that is) but
    thankfully
quit before she met me,
'cause there are two things that really set my teeth on edge:
people who do drugs,
and people who reminisce
about doing drugs,
even weed,
are gross,
but that's just me,
a girl who dabbled and quit immediately thereafter, uppers and
    downers,
they fucked up my head so much, even a line
of coke transported me into the familiar organ,
the sad, dark spleen, so all right
I may be a bit jealous
of those who have the two things I don't:
a steel stomach
and a stable head, Pasha stays away
from all that shit, we have that in common,
Nadya still thinks coke
is kind of cool, it's part of her Moscow glamour past,
but I know she would never do it
as long as she's with me, Nadyenka
can make an oath that could outlive
the fall of this empire if it's
for me, Pasha
used to be high
all the time, you'd never guess it,
he could go to work at the lab,
or pick up some groceries, all the while
he was totally gone, that was
years ago, and then he just
stopped, cold turkey,
and he never touched an opioid
ever again, not even
over-the-counter painkillers, I guess Nadya and Pasha
had that in common,
their toughened

will, the thing is
Pashenka always had something in him, when he was ten
he tried to hang himself, not to
die, but to get
very close to death, he had this friend at the time,
Martin, he grew up in Chicago and only had
a mom, Martin and Pasha
had that boyhood type of love,
they annoyed the shit out of each other and couldn't live
without the other, Martin admired Pasha I think,
or he sort of followed his lead, it was Pasha's idea
that Martin would help him
hang himself, so that Pasha could
graze the edge
of his last breath, and just then
Martin would free him, it could have gone
very wrong, but Pasha lived,
and Martin moved to a school in Detroit
four years later, his mama got with
a new man, they both hit puberty
in different ways, they stopped
messaging, Pasha still has
a little bit of the imprint on the side
of his neck, it's where he tattooed
a kitten, something all three of us
had in common, we loved
cats,

all three of us
drank champagne, we danced
to Zemfira of course, who gave a concert at the Music Media
    Dome in Moscow
the day of the Russian invasion of Ukraine
(forbidden to refer to it as a 'war' in Russia)
if you went to her website,
all it said was
*Nyet Voynye*
*No To War*, shortly after,
she was out of the country, she lives in Paris now
with her partner, the Russian filmmaker Renata Litvinova,

Renata with her Golden Age of Cinema look,
blonde finger-wave bob and starlet brows, and Zemfira,
that small androgynous build with eyes pinched and tilted, perhaps
    ever-forgiving,
underneath her black tussled hair, rock and roll baby, I was also
    living
in Paris, slicking
my hair for elegance,
knuckle tats for push-back, so yes,
when I moved to Berlin for good, Nadya and I sort of thought
(I'm embarrassed to say)
that we were the poor-man's version
of them, or it gave us a dream-world,
we also wanted to fall out of the era,
and we had guts and beauty, so we danced
to Zemfira, and I imagined how Renata would kiss her
in private,
on the balcony of a five-star hotel room,
paparazzi hidden in the bushes, the Hôtel Plaza Athénée
on Avenue Montaigne, or the Cheval Blanc
on the Quai du Louvre, or who knows
where celebrities stay, I just need some details for my avatar,
    Nadyenka and I
would kiss in private, on the balcony of a five-star hotel room,
paparazzi hidden in the bushes, the Hôtel Plaza Athénée
on Avenue Montaigne, or the Cheval Blanc
the Quai du Louvre, or both,
in our white fleece bathrobes
with the Eiffel Tower shimmering against the violet sky, I told
    Nadyenka
I never felt pretty, it was Soviet
anti-Semitism, it's not that Nadya doesn't have empathy,
she has tons of empathy, but she was starting to tilt her eyes
in that way that said,
You can't blame everything on Soviet
anti-Semitism, I'm not trying to get high off Soviet
anti-Semitism, I don't need her to understand
what it's like to be an ugly Jew, 'cause I know
what it's like to be an ugly Jew, in these conversations
I felt so indignant that my heels and my palms burnt, I'd rather

destroy the world
than forgive it,

Pasha dances alone a lot,
even when he is dancing with someone, he closes
his eyes and he is
in the cosmos, he is
a planet made of water,

it was dark in Berlin, on Ilsestraße, fifth floor, last year,
after we danced to Zemfira, I put on
Angel Ulyanov's 'Davai Zamutim', which Nadya wasn't a fan of,
    the song itself
wasn't my thing either, but I loved
that tall, skeletal queer kid,
head shaved and a crown of thorns tattooed on his skull, and I
    loved the video,
though I know it's a bit simple and righteous, but it's pretty damn
    daring
for Russia (part of those years of great hope,
the Russian Renaissance that was simmering,
artists, queers, clubs, cultural spaces, literature, magazines,
Brezhnev's *glasnost* part two, Pussy
Riot performing 'A Punk Prayer' inside Moscow's Cathedral of
    Christ the Saviour,
and all that stuff that made it into the *New York Times*,
and all the stuff that didn't,
the gays and lezzies and bis and non-binaries and trans,
the freaks, gentle and headstrong, the ones not just from Moscow
    but
from Norilsk above the Arctic Circle,
from Siberian Krasnoyarsk on the Yenisei,
the Volga Tatars from Bashkortostan,
Armenians, Mongols,
from Chernyshevsky in Sakha,
Plesetsk, Tikhvin, sure Saint Pete,
you get the picture), Angel's video
is a group of *gopniki*, shaved-head street-thug types, all Adidas and
    sharp cheekbones,
walking the desolate city, wire fencing and concrete, they go

down into the metro
and there's Angel dressed like he doesn't belong there,
the gang approaches, it's Fag Beat-Down O'Clock,
the ringleader lifts his hand and,
out of nowhere, starts voguing, you can't say
it's not a little awesome,
*Davai Zamutim* means Let's Start Something, and we did
start something, no one
would have guessed that it'd all come to a halt
on 24 February,
when Russia invaded the Ukrainian capital, and the city where
I was born on the north-east border, and don't get me started
on how happening Kyiv was,
up-and-coming queer and all that,
and despite the severe corruption
(which no post-Soviet territory was rid of)
clubs like Cxema and Rhythm Büro,
raves and DIY parties
in office blocks, disused factories, skate parks,
*VESELKA* (Ukrainian for rainbow),
gay, kinky, platonic, poly, sober, the new wave of a new world,
it wasn't about getting pissed and gone, it was about
honouring the lifeblood
of the throwaways,
the debris of imperialism,
the extinct animals of the Ottoman Empire
and Tatars fallen from the noble towers,
the pockmarked ravines of Western Ukraine where the *Einsatzgruppen*
combed bullets
into the Jewish hair,
the dissidents and gays, piled,
and the locals who helped,
all that blood rises
and moves to the beat,
Pasha in the U-Bahn
wearing his black tee with *Pyedor* written on the back,
meaning Faggot,
underneath his zip-up brown-and-blue jacket,
Pasha was a faggot,
and I was a dyke,

and I was a faggot,
and Pasha was a dyke,

he finished his glass of champagne and went for
his shoes, zipped up his
brown-and-blue jacket, *Poka lyubimiye*,
he said, Goodbye, my loves, he had
a midnight kiss waiting for him
in Rudow, Who lives in Rudow?
I asked, The man, Pasha said,
of my dreams,

there's this joke,
and it goes like this:
Brezhnev meets Sophia Loren
(his eyes drivel underneath those bushy brows)
and he tells her,
Ms Loren, allow me to grant you any wish you desire,
at which Sophia Loren replies with those plump Roma lips,
I want you
to let
anyone
who wants to leave the Soviet Union
leave the Soviet Union,
Brezhnev shuffles his cheeks,
a chunk of hair comes out of his wax-combed general 'do, he
    replies,
Sophia,
you sly little minx,
you just want to be alone with me,

in 1991, a ship in a bottle
known as the USSR, the bottle
shattered, and the ship
set out to sea, the flood
of immigrants with visas and official stamps
of the international guilty conscience washed in,
I left far west for America,
and Nadyenka left near west for Germany,

Ukraine became independent, and
was the first ex-Soviet country to remove
its sodomy laws
(I like to make the causality, why not),
free Ukraine,
my Ukraine,
beloved Ukraine,
Jew-hating Ukraine,
you never
claimed me as your own
until I left,

it snowed
in Berlin a little in November, and melted the same day, it snowed
    again
last week and held on
till morning, Nadyenka and I haven't taken our bikes out
since that Deutschland cold stiffed up the air,
they sit double-locked in the building courtyard,
right below the ground-floor window
of the couple with two cats, one brown-and-black Maine Coon and
    one short-haired pure-white kitty, they
come to the window every time they hear the jangle
of a bike lock being released, they press their wet noses, wanting to
    know the world,
Nadyenka and I extra-jangled our keys and purses and whatever it
    was that could jangle,
and sometimes the owners, the young couple who live on the
    ground floor,
came to the window annoyed,
and we had to quickly bend and hank ourselves into position,
holding onto the handlebars or bike wheel, unlocking each lock as
    if we hadn't even noticed that there were cats, in truth,
there were days when there was nothing but chasing cats, October
was particularly sweet, though the trees were already bare, the trees
lose their leaves much earlier in Berlin than in Paris, I don't know
    why,
the hairlessness of woodland always pains me,
the day is long

enough as it is, harsh winds
snuff out the noise in my head, but still
waiting at the light at Gielower Straße
(I was running errands – the term I used
to legitimise my wandering),
the light turned green, God
knows why, I stood still
at the curb and closed my eyes and thought, for two years
– it was
1915 and 1916 –
they sent
all those Armenians
into the Syrian desert
to die,

wet leaves
are really good for me, the way they plaster together, the veins in
    their sodden bodies
webbing each other, over-moist
and split, they gob the gutters and coat the sidewalks,
you have to watch
where you're going, and I was practising
being outside
when I'm outside,
looking outwards has always been hard, that's the thing
about me,
or people like me,
is that we really do
want help,

November was so-so,
though there was a week in the beginning full of promise,
that's when we last unlocked our pair of *velosipedov*, lingered our faces
at the whiskers behind the glass of the ground-floor window, and
    rode north
to Prenzlauer Berg,
my bike was a used white Kettler, I named it *zaichik* (bunny), Nadyenka
    had found it for me on eBay Kleinanzeigen (a German eBay to
    sell your stuff and buy
someone else's stuff), it was a present

before my arrival in Berlin, her bike was black,
a taped-up Rehberg she called Harley (like Harley Davidson),
she even scraped it up a bit more
with an old nail file
she was going to toss anyways,
it was so no one would steal it, You shouldn't have anything that
    looks too good,
Nadya said, unless you're willing to lose it,
it was a long bike ride,
a laborious one, I didn't particularly like
going to Prenzlauer Berg, Nadya biked too fast,
and I always missed the red lights she licked,
and when I did keep up she kept turning her head to fawn over the
    weird face I made
when I cycled, I didn't like
all that attention and speed,

back during the Cold
War, the East Berliners were called *Ossi*, from the German word
    for east (Ost),
and the West Berliners were called, you guessed it,
from the German word for west, *Wessi*, and each had their own tropes,
the Ossi were lazy, ambitionless, bitter, and self-pitying,
the Wessi, full of it, pushy, smug, and spoon-fed,
Funny,
I wanted to say to Nadya, a dry side-comment,
how in the Soviet Union,
we only had one type of person who was all those things:
Jews,
but I just made a note of it in my head, I'd tell it
to my Ashkenazi Ukrainian friend Klarochka,
she'd get it,

Klarochka had a job in London, an NGO
that connected Jewish communities in Europe
to legal resources (in short), she was really into her job,
and always up for a talk about Jews,
but her Semitic stamina
out-did mine far and wide, and then I
started to get annoyed with Klara, God, I thought,

all she talks about
is Jews,

the writer Sholem Aleichem
was brought up often in my household, my mamachka loved
that Ukrainian Yiddish humourist, as did all of Ukraine, as did all
    of Russia,
(even a grade-A Slavic anti-Semite had one Jew writer they adored),
Aleichem said something about
it being a hideous, cruel world
and that the only way to get back at it
was by laughing,

Nadyenka
and I locked our bikes together
on Auguststraße and went into the cramped Holy Grail
bookstore
of fashion and arts publications,
we paged through the limited-edition magazines, Japanese quartos,
    select interviews, heavy art catalogues, a ringed Codex folio,
    morphed text on a glossy volume, photo collections printed on
    delicate paper or coarse sheets, matte or ridged sugar paper,
    wrapped in translucent calque, covers like aluminium foil,
    iridescent rainbow scales from the reflecting overhead light,
we thumbed and flipped and paged
and closed each book
and put it back in its place,
we go there
to buy nothing, just to feel
around and gawk
and dream, and me,
I also stroked my ego, I pointed out
the issues where I had a short story published,
since I had short stories published
in some of these super-cool issues, but
there was always a thorn in my mood, a private one,
where I thought, if I'm published in these super-cool magazines, why
can't I afford to buy books
in this super-cool bookstore? it began to drizzle,
a humid vapour, odd for November, but that November was odd,

Nadya and I held each other in the street outside the shop,
as if we were waiting to see
if it would turn into rain, or pass all together,
I snuck my nose
into the collar of her puffy jacket, I think that's where I felt the thorn
that I did not share with Nadya, nor later with Klara, I left
a wet trace from my runny nose on the nylon shoulder,
by the time I separated my head
from her body, the drizzle
had died out,

it was last February, on the couch of my apartment in Paris,
I was making out with Nadya real sloppy,
it had been just a couple of days
since the war began, my mama called me
and I felt around for the phone
to turn it off
but ended up opening the call, Mama told me
that she didn't want to rattle me, but
Europe is as good as gone,
Russian soldiers had taken Chernobyl and its reactors,
she was on speaker phone,
she said that her and my dad would pay for my flight home,
What flight? Nadya mouthed next to me,
Mama had many points to make,
which were the same point many times,
I need to think about it all, I can't
just make these types of decisions
on the spot, I said,
Yes, she said, of course
think about it, but don't think about it
too long, things move fast,

remember what Baba Vanga said,

Vangeliya Pandeva Gushterova,
or Baba Vanga,
the Bulgarian mystic my mama cross-referenced CNN with
was born premature and deemed unlikely to survive, her father
got called into the Bulgarian army during World War I, her mother

died soon after,
the war finished and her father came back,
but their home is now on territory ceded to Yugoslavia
and her father is shortly arrested
for pro-Bulgarian activities, their family
property
is seized by the government,
he's released,
they make ends meet,
twelve-year-old Vangeliya is playing with her cousins when
a dust storm hits,
a tornado
sweeps her body
off the ground
and young Vangeliya disappears,
the storm settles,
no one can find Vangeliya, the family friends send out
a search party, they comb and they yell,
Vangeliiiiyaa, Vangeeeelllllliiiiyyyyyaaaa,
the sun switches sides,
Vangeliiiiyaa, Vangeeeelllllliiiiyyyyyaaaa,
in the forest, they find a girl
with her eyes swollen and sealed
with sand and dust,
it was
Vangeliya,
she was
blinded
by the storm,
the doctors tried
to save her sight, but it was gone
for good,
except that,
she had developed
a new sight,
a second sight,
a vision
of the future,
she gave revelations to the locals that turned out
to be true,

exactly true, people started coming from afar,
by the 1980s
she had given thousands of accurate predictions,
and became known as the 'Nostradamus of the Balkans',
suspicious scientists came to test her,
high-ranking officials and leaders from Soviet Republics
(like Brezhnev)
came to seek her advice,
she foresaw major events
like 9/11, the 2004 tsunami, Barack Obama's victory, Brexit,
a lot,
the ones that occupied my mamachka's mind
during that phone call
were about the future of Europe and Russia, Baba Vanga predicted
that by 2025 Europe will no longer be inhabited
and that World War III will come and, as a result,
Russia will dominate the world,
and in 2076, Communism will return to Europe and the rest of
    the world,
a timely forecast,
But, Mama,
I reminded her, Baba Vanga also said
that in 2130, with the help of aliens, we will live underwater,
Yes, my mama said,
but that's later,

when I got off the phone, Nadya and I
weren't feeling so horny anymore,
Are you going to go to America? Nadya asked,
she couldn't come with me,
not with her Russian passport,
her parents had insisted on all three of them keeping
the Russian passport
all these years,
because Germany didn't allow dual nationality,
and just the suggestion of rethinking the paperwork
brought tears to Nadyenka's eyes, I can't
turn my back on Russia, But it's just a passport, I said,
You wouldn't understand, Nadya was biting her lower lip,
but I had a chip on my shoulder about allegiance as well,

feeling awfully homesick
for a country I never really knew, having left
Ukraine at seven, I kept making sweeping life
decisions in the late hours of drab Sundays,
about giving it all up and moving back to Ukraine,
free Ukraine,
my beloved Ukraine,
and I would call up my mama, and say, Mama,
I want to go back to Ukraine,
free Ukraine,
my beloved Ukraine,
I think it's always been my home,
my mama
would cut into my declaration
*Upasi Bozhé,* Not a chance, baby, Ukraine
is a broken country, No, it's not, I argued,
You don't know what the new Kyiv's like, it's a renaissance,
and gay-friendly, and there are jobs,
Mama sighed, The east is a two-faced muse, she mumbled,
(it's a shit-show, she was trying to say)
corruption up to the chin,
and I know she's right,
but I have legal papers for two continents now
and I'm still lost,
Your generation, my mama continued, is really hooked on the pathos
    of motherland,
Mama, you had somewhere to put your feet,
but my feet are still hovering,
I climbed back on top of Nadyenka
and ran each finger along her eyebrows,
I'm not going
anywhere
without you,

there's this joke,
and it goes like this:
Ivan Ivanovich
arrives fresh to the Gulag
with his sprouty twenty years of age,
and a square-faced long-timer says, Hey, kid, how long you in for?

Three years, says Ivan,
Three years, the old man looks him up and down, What for?
For nothing . . . sighs Ivan,
Don't lie to me, kid, the rough-skinned prisoner huffs,
everybody knows 'for nothing' is five years,

at the time Nadyenka opened up her mailbox and took out the
    police report
I was living in Paris, in a different apartment near Gare de Lyon, single
and ready to mingle, not yet diagnosed,
freestyle in my untrustworthy mind,
not a milligram of medication to brace me, a drunkard
without a drop of liquor, wandering dyke parties at night,
the hole-in-the-wall near the Pompidou museum, at Chez Maxime's,
    Rosa Bonheur,
Yoyo, that new green structure across the Seine, the dingy bar near
    the Voltaire metro,
and shuffling my feet around pigeon-shat parks during the day,
ending up at Jardin Villemin off Canal Saint-Martin,
I chain smoked in broken footpaths, much like a pigeon
amongst the other pigeons,

during the week I went to work
and sat with horrible posture,
answered the phone, took minutes, filed, copied, scheduled, and
    daydreamed
about a woman to love,

Nadezhda
had met her ex-wife at a club in Moscow,
her parents kept their apartment there and so the family went
    regularly,
Nadya had been a true teenage Berliner, giving her emigré parents
    a good sweat
with all-nighters who-knows-where, and phone calls from who-
    knows-who
blaring those Neue Deutsche Welle CDs, post-punk rock and new
    wave,
banging around her bedroom to the '80s West-Berlin dyke-wet-
    dream girl-group, Malaria!

till something clicked and she fell in love with the Moscow-
    scene,
and with Slavic girls, who she told me fucked the best,
the only Slavic girl I've fucked has been Nadezhda,
so I think she's right,
I don't know if it's about
the type of fucking that comes out of the Soviet Union,
I'd never been fucked the way Nadezhda's fucked me, but I'd also
    never been
bathed the way that Nadezhda's bathed me, I never had
a lover pronounce my name the way it was given to me at birth,
with all the Russian sounds in pitch,
I've said I love you and I have been told I love you,
I've said *Je t'aime* and have been told *Je t'aime*,
but I've never had a woman look at me
and see
who I was without my body,
and tell me the phrase I had waited
for a country to say to me,
*Ya lyublyu tebya*
in my language
my free language,
my beloved language,
I love you – *Ya lyublyu tebya*,
the way Anna Karenina said it to Vronsky,
or Dr Zhivago to Lara Antipova,
or the Master to Margarita,
I said it back to Nadyenka,
and between us
centuries of Slavic loves
and death, between us, the Romanov family
are woken up in the middle of the night,
taken to a twenty-by-sixteen-foot basement
and shot, and between us,
Lenin's bust glimmers from the podium light
at Taras Shevchenko National University of Kyiv, and between us,
a woman who is nearing 100 years old
has moved her chair to the doorway, away from the window,
in a nursing home in Chaiky village in Kyiv,
shards rain from the sky,

between us a seventeen-year-old girl
walks the streets of Soviet Kharkov, picking up
unexploded shells and ammunition with her bare hands,
between us,
the city is empty of men,
the rest are evacuated, women stuff children against their hips,
their children and other's children,
so that each small face has a stomach to press against
on a long train ride to Uzbekistan, Nadyenka tells me,
*Ya lyublyu tebya*, and all the unmarked
graves
grow names,

Nadya mentioned that sex
with her ex-wife
wasn't that frequent,
and then ceased all together the last two years,
she was never that into it, Nadyenka added,
I couldn't help but circle the question
of how Nadezhda made it those five years with her,
she was a very sexual person,
had even thought about being an escort,
said she could be good at it, I think
she'd be amazing at it, I told her, she's got those natural skills,
tactile way of looking, listening, speaking, but, she said,
I want to be all yours,
I knew I was naively glamourising
what was a real job,
and had friends who were sex workers,
but I don't think it was about the sex, it was about
her Russianness,
about the way I had always
been scared of Russian women,
their feline features,
decorative ulterior motives,
stern beauty regimens,
iron gender and high cheekbones,
Pushkin's Tatyana Larina, Dostoevsky's Nastasya Filippovna,
Soviet Darwin's,
graceful subjugators, fiancée-ready, chauvinist flirts,

effortlessly patriotic and paranoid of all other women,
with that lock-and-key devotion
to the wrong man, always
wrong men,
the ruthless commandant female,
breast milk, menstruation, broken hymen,
and the intoxication of maleness, the *muschina* pheromones,
the way these women looked at me,
my Jewish nose and Ukrainian mediocrity,
the distance I took from men, the sexlessness in my gaze,
I carried their scrutiny to the West, to North America, to Europe,
to my bedroom,
to every part of a woman
I put in my mouth, I was terrified
of these lady comrades,
and yet, I was blatant and impervious
with every other kind of woman, American, French, you name it,
putty to my quick wit and my masterful way of taking distance,
I think I became that Russian Brutus (Brutuslava?),
and was power-boozed with all the qualities
that tyrannised me,
(I understand the etymology of their behaviour,
martial socialism doesn't bode well for gender,
the savant pianist, chess champion, mathematician and the last of
    Slavic export:
the female), I imagined Nadezhda,
who was no doubt a dyke, a Berliner, but also
Russian,
a real Russian woman,
who wanted to make me come,
the Machiavellian vamp
who would show me how deformed and mediocre
I was,
(I can't quite say it's a kink,
or perhaps not fully fledged),
when I told Nadya
that I'm scared of Russian women,
she said,
me too,

her ex-wife was tall and angular,
brown eyes, short hair,
the type of gait that would once be called 'a rock-star walk'
but soon revealed itself to just be the childish footing
of a slouchy girl from Chelyabinsk,
(famous for its tank production
and that asteroid that hit in 2013,
which is now on display
at the Regional Museum, that's something,
at least for the region)
she had studied to be a graphic designer and come to Moscow
for the jobs (and the women),
had the girls chasing her signature moody boyish manners, till one
    came her way
and wouldn't let her go,
and every dyke from the East knows
a girl from the West is worth holding on to,

it is dark,
black-milk dark,
in the black-milk darkness of our bedroom on Ilsestraße, fifth floor,
it is the first day of winter, Nadezhda
and I are sitting
knee to knee,
she has lowered her shoulders,
it's the darkest hour
of the darkest day,
there is a chill,
it's the open window,
we don't close it, we sit
knee to knee,
Nadyenka lifts her hand
from her lap and stretches her index finger to her eye,
maybe there's an eyelash that has curved into her iris,
or a fleck of something airborne,
or just a twitch of a nerve, she bends her other fingers
and rubs her knuckle in slow curves into the socket,
but when the knuckle leaves her eye, she blinks,
a couple times,

to smooth over her sight,
I don't understand why
it matters so much to me,
my diaphragm bends and my belly tightens,
because it matters so much to me, to know
what it was, a twisted eyelash,
a particle of dust, a nerve spasm,
a memory,
I don't know what she's thinking,


Nadezhda met her ex-wife at *the* Moscow club, to be precise,
the Solyanka Club, off the Barrikadnaya metro,
the hippest low-key high-key cosmopolitan oasis,
part-restaurant, part-art space, part-music mecca,
the place had a designer clothes shop and a gallery with a special
    selection of pieces, its own magazine, and movie nights, the way
    Nadya talked about it, I thought
fuck
is Moscow where it was always happening, I wasn't a nightlife
    person at all,
the state of my mental health (or lack thereof) preventing me from
    drinking too much or taking any drugs – all I could do was
    smoke cigarettes, and boy did I smoke
and use the club space to air out my melancholia –
but going out and having a blast, I never got the hang of that, the
    way Nadyenka described going out in Moscow,
all these years,
I started to wonder, could I have used my nights
in a completely different way? no one
explained to me that the night
was not just for sadness,


there was also Simachev Bar (owned by Denis Simachev,
the bling fashion designer, who spun imperial, revolutionary and
    Soviet codes into street wear), it was a posh spot, central, a brisk
    walk
from the Kremlin and Red Square, off the Kuznetsky Most stop,
it had Simachev's designer boutique on the first floor,
and then the restaurant and the club, open twenty-four hours,
some say, forget Solyanka, the best parties were at Simachev,

but Nadya says, You can't love one parent more than another,
(though Pasha would say, Sure you can)
and Nadya did love those two spots as if they raised her,
My grandma, Nadyenka said, it was her mother's mom,
was getting sicker and sicker in Moscow,
and my mom was always chasing me away
from the apartment
and then telling me I was a spoiled good-for-nothing daughter
who couldn't even take time
to care for her family,
but no one could be around her mother,
she snapped nerves, popped blood vessels,
but when I had lunches and dinners with her,
she was nothing but nice (which was confusing),
You have to believe me, Nadyenka pleaded, she's not what she
    seems,
and I did,
of course I did,
I believe you, Nadya,
my Nadyenka, my Nadezhda,
my Hope,
but not always,

She insisted that she had forgiven her mother for all of that, she
looked at me flat-cast, and the subject was closed,
Berlin is Berlin, Nadya said,
and I was a teenager, I was happy
to be out of the apartment,
to get dressed and lacquer up,
but Moscow was different, Simachev was like walking into
both a new and old Russia, half ironic, half style-gorged,
with cherry-coloured hair salon chairs, a mirror-tiled sink counter
    rimmed in gold, red velvet curtains with camel fringe, a chandelier
    above the DJ stage,
there's more, Nadyenka scattered the details
and my imagination began to redecorate,
the music was apparently the best, no matter the genre,
funk, house, hip-hop or cheesy Russian pop,
both spots have since closed, and there was still Propaganda
    Club,

a converted traditional Russian restaurant on Bolshoy Zlatoustinsky
    Lane,
It's cool but it's not the same, Nadya sighed,

things like this always happen to her,
these 'no way' things,
she saw her ex-wife – literally – across the room
in Solyanka, at that time Nadya was with another girl
who had come down from Saint Pete, where she lived,
to spend the weekend with Nadya,
We weren't dating really,
just spending time together, Nadyenka smiled,
there was something cruel in her words,
I knew she was not a cruel person, but the nettle
in her description of the poor girl
who took the near-four-hour train to see her
only to be left on the dance floor
for a mystery-charmer
leaning a bit smug against the bar,
making eyes at Nadyenka,
and Nadyenka's clear eyes flashing white in the disco light,
There was nothing to be done, Nadya went on,
but go to her, and, as soon as I went to her,
it was destiny,
and that was that, though Nadyenka spun the story so that
at times it was destiny
and at others it was her fault,
but the past is written, she left her Saint Pete *podruga*
who wasn't really her *podruga*, and got a new *podruga*
who she took back with her to Berlin
and married,

our destiny
had started two years ago (okay, nineteen months), not that long,
and not that short, but between us
two thousand years at least, it had been
two years and a couple of months since the divorce when we met,
and it was an instant thing, not necessarily love-at-first-sight,
to be honest, I wasn't initially enamoured
with Nadyenka's exterior, I wasn't not enamoured, just

it was something else that connected between us, way before
our bodies connected, that type of feeling,
well, a couple of years back, I would have proposed something
    impulsive,
a shotgun wedding,
but now the paperwork alone – Nadyenka knows better than
    anyone
divorces are expensive,
But we're not going to get divorced, Nadya insisted,
we're going to grow old together,
Nadya stated as pure, scientific fact,
my nervous system flagged these types of comments
as terrible judgement,
unrealistic projections,
though my therapist reminded me
that sometimes I take things a bit literally,
and people can use words
not to put forth facts
but to make wishes,
and, in truth, I wanted
what she wanted, but my wanting
had a bad track record, I wanted
so badly
to grow old with her,
I couldn't wait for her to brush my wiry grey hair,
and how we would each be stationed in our kitchen,
her cutting beetroot, me cutting the onions (I always volunteered)
    and peeling the boiled eggs
for the *selyotka pod shuboi*, the name meaning herring under a fur
    coat,
the heavy multi-layered salad with chopped earthy potatoes, crunchy
    root vegetables and sweet beets covering the briny small fish
(I didn't even particularly like herring, but in my fantasy I want us
    to be making this salad because it takes time and attention and
    Nadyenka loves herring)
the fantasy turned into us preparing an intimate New Year's feast,
    with orange-red caviar, smoked sardine *shproti*, *Olivye* salad with
    cubes of pickles and potatoes and egg and sausage with canned
    peas (and carrots – not everyone added, but we did) and gobs
    of mayonnaise,

when Nadyenka made it for me, she added carrots too,
she made a spectacular *Olivye*
(though not as good as my papa's, the only person to beat my papa's
    *Olivye*
was my prababushka Gala,
but my papa used her recipe),
I, of course, didn't tell Nadyenka that my papa made it better,
as I'm sure she didn't tell me that her mama
made it better, she was an amazing cook
and an awful mom, according to Nadya,
in our old age, I could see
exactly where Nadyenka's skin would fold and sag,
though she said she wouldn't let it get that far,
she had already consulted her dermatologist, Tatyana,
who was a Moldav woman with great insight into preventative
    skincare,
My forehead is too small for Botox, Nadyenka explained,
Tatyana said that deadening the nerves there would make my brow
    sag,
(and Nadyenka prided herself on her brow bones,
I thought they were a work of art too,
I'm sure if her skull was found by future alien archaeologists,
the ones who eventually help us build an underwater civilisation,
they would 'oh' and 'ah' at the sculpture of bone around her eye
    sockets),

I saw Nadyenka's Russianness, the Russianness that scared me,
and lured me,
it was in her skincare routine,
she owns an ultra-sound collagen-stimulating gadget,
and a hand-held electric skin-toning device with the two noddles
    that sends little shocks into the skin to stimulate elasticity, she
    tried it on me,
and it felt great actually, a little tingly,
but mainly great
to feel like I have this power over time and gravity,
Nadyenka kept up with multiple beauty vlogs from some Russians
    and Ukrainians,
someone named Kira who had immigrated to London,
she'd been following Kira for so many years

that she saw how difficult it was for her to get pregnant,
and the healthy birth of her child,
and the death of her first dog
(a fluff-haired chihuahua named Denna,
I miss Dennochka, Nadya lamented),
and there was another vlogger from Luhansk who didn't emigrate,
she's still in Ukraine, Olesya,
doing her vlogs from her bedroom or the mall or her hair salon,
and sometimes she films herself walking out of her apartment
    complex to the salon,
and we can see some of the streets are cracked and taped off,
and behind her sirens whirl, and she says, Oy, it's so noisy here,
but she never talks about the war,
Nadyenka says she's glad that Olesya
doesn't say anything about all that,
'Cause why can't we just talk about hair and make-up, why does
    war have to make
geopolitical correspondents of us all?
I like Olesya, she has some sort of lisp,
her lips crossed a bit off-centre with certain vowels,
and her hair is over-dyed auburn, and she has a little extra on her
    waist,
she holds each product in her long-manicured two fingers
and lifts them towards the camera
with such reverence,
each container and the application of its contents is a holy act,
for the dusting of powder to the tap, tap of under-eye cream,
to the thumb pressed downwards from the temple to drain the
    lymph nodes, she is devout
and remarkably non-judgemental,
on one vlog she did make-up on a trans woman, Kalyna,
copper-toned hair tucked behind her ears,
and effervescent eyes with dark lashes fanning at the lens,
Kalynochka, what a beauty you are,
Olesya turned her face gently to the light,
we watched that one together, Nadyenka and I,
so proud to see Kalynochka on the vlog,
being treated with such care, Nadya told me,
Don't scroll down,
I scrolled down,

there was a plunging list of comments, Nadyenka said,
Don't read them,
I read them,
the same old words, sticks and stones,
knives and guns,
rape and murder,
I'm tired of reading bloodthirst,
but Olesya didn't take the video down,
she just deleted as many of them as she could
(though they kept coming), and even had Kalynochka on for another
    episode
(the theme that time was a disco look), I mentioned it to my friends
    in Paris,
they were sincerely concerned, but it wasn't the communion I
    needed,
only Nadyenka and I could sit
and watch Olesya and Kalynochka
and just know
what didn't need words,
Kalynochka,
our beloved Kalynochka,
and the warmth of Nadyenka's head
on my thigh, as she curled up to my knees
and I caressed the skin behind her ear,
as Olesya spun Kalynochka on the hair salon chair,
serenading her
with blessings,

there's this joke, here it is:
We are now entering day 269
of the special military operation
to take Kyiv
in two days,

even if
Baba Vanga predicted Russia's worldwide domination,
it wouldn't happen as quick as Putin had boasted,
the subject of those pesky Ukrainian fascists had to have been a
    blow to his ego,
a Russian man

will give up everything
his money,
his leg,
even his son,
before . . .

Yakov Iosifovich Dzhugashvili,
otherwise Yasha,
was the son of a Georgian woman by the name of Ekaterine
    Svanidze, otherwise Kato,
and a Georgian man by the name of Ioseb Besarionis dze
    Dzhugashvili, otherwise
Joseph Stalin,
(it was the fashion, even Vladimir Ilyich Ulyanov
changed his name to Lenin,
for one of the three reasons historians still argue over:

one,
from the etymology of the term meaning 'a large river' (possibly a
    party inside joke),
two,
he signed his early essays, starting from 1901, with 'N Lenin',
    which coincidently was not long after a covert trip he made out
    of the country with the passport a friend had lent him of her
    deceased father named Nikolay Egorovich Lenin – the date of
    birth adjusted,
three,
a big fan of Tolstoy, Vladimir Ilyich Ulyanov borrowed the
    protagonist from his novel *The Cossacks*, Olenin, who's sentenced
    to hard labour in the Caucasus, but ends up falling in love with
    a life free of 'high-society')
Dzhugashvili was dropped for Stalin,
'the man of steel',
the material that described best not only his political sangfroid
but also his style of paternal care,
Yasha
was his eldest child, the son of his first wife, and Stalin made it known
that he could not take care of Yasha
because he had a revolution to raise,
when Yasha was fourteen,

his father had already become the star of the Bolshevik government,
and then the Soviet Union, Yasha was timid,
a self-conscious young man,
with a solemn brow and Georgian crown to his lip
(just some of the qualities that infuriated the man of steel),
his father also clarified their relations, he forbade Yasha from
    changing his last family name to Stalin,
Yasha fell madly in love with an Orthodox priest's daughter,
he brought her home (to Stalin's dacha) to meet his father,
Stalin showed up, looked at the girl, and expressed his opinion
with his temper,
the fiancée ran out of the house, Stalin slammed the door behind
    her,
Yasha got the pistol, turned the barrel to his heart
and fired,
but the handle slipped,
and the bullet pierced his lung instead,
Stalin told his ex-wife, Kato, that it's no surprise, the boy lacked
lustre and was depressive from birth, Yasha woke up
in the hospital with a patched lung, he later married the girl
he had wanted to marry, together they had a daughter
born on a blanket of snow on the seventh day of February,
Yasha fawned madly over her,
eight months later the infant
died of pneumonia, his marriage
didn't make it to two years,
to give his lousy son
something to do, Stalin booted him to the military,
Yasha was sent to the front,
and, following his luck,
Operation Barbarossa came to a head at exactly that moment,
the Nazi troops pushed through the Soviet border, a matter of
    weeks and
Yasha and his fellow soldiers of the Twentieth Army were captured
    in Belorussia,
he tried to escape,
but was caught and brought back,
it was his military brethren, the Red Army fellows,
who ratted him out as Stalin's son,
which gave the Nazis

an idea,
they had no plan to torture him,
in fact, they treated him with more respect and care
than his own father,
Hitler drafted a message for Stalin, stating
they were in possession of a Red Army lieutenant
(lieutenant being the lowest rank of a commissioned officer)
who happened to be his son, Yakov
Dzhugashvili,
and that, if he wanted that boy alive,
they would need a swap,
more specifically, the German
Field Marshal Friedrich Paulus
(marshal being the most senior military rank),
who had been taken prisoner in Stalingrad months prior,
time was ticking, and the pressure was on, Yasha
was sent to the Sachsenhausen concentration camp
in Oranienburg, less than an hour north of Berlin,
where he waited for the father
he had waited for
his whole life,
Stalin got the note,
thought about it,
and drafted his own response,
which would later become
one of his best-known phrases:

*I do not trade field marshals for lieutenants,*

two weeks after his thirty-sixth birthday,
Yasha was executed,
it was Pasha
who told me the whole story
(don't think I'm so erudite in Soviet military history),
I think he related terribly to Yasha,
he especially took his time recounting the last part,
Yasha at the camp,
apparently, he tried to escape there too,
and one of the Nazi guardsmen caught him under his nose
and raised his gun at Yashenka

and Yasha turned around and hooked his eyes to the guard's
and cried out with broken voice,
Shoot, shoot,
but the guard stared back and his grip loosened
and he lowered
the gun, Pasha said
he couldn't shoot a man
with fatherless eyes, Yasha,
Yashyenka,
Pasha's beloved Yakov,
Pasha said
boys like him were stillborn,
they never had a chance,
but surely absolute misfortune cannot be, I argued,
someone's destiny,

Pasha shrugged,

there's this joke, and it goes
like this: Nurse, the young man says,
where are we going?
To the morgue, the nurse answers,
But, nurse,
the young man says,
I haven't died yet!
Well,
the nurse places her palm gently on his shoulder,
we haven't arrived yet,

I don't want to talk about Pasha
with Nadezhda, she tells me
we should
talk about it,
it would
help me,
I get furious and I'm afraid to say it,
that Nadya wants to help me more
than I want to be helped,
on our way to Kaufland to get more white onions for Nadya to
   marinade in her jars,

and the rest she'd fry up with mushrooms (wild, if they have them,
    shiitake, or if nothing else, button mushrooms) and potatoes
    with dill for her signature *zharenaya kartoshka*,
we hold hands and with our free ones we hold
rolled-up grocery bags,
and I know that I've cut off my step
and I'm glazing over, nose to the crowd stepping out of the U-Bahn
    and I'm seeing
a boy
scratching his neck and he lowers
his hand and there's
a colourful kitten
tattoo peeling
on his throat,

last summer, the U-Bahn and trains were packed,
the German government offered up a nine-euro monthly transport
    ticket
that you could use on buses, U- and S-Bahns, trams, local and
    regional trains,
and so everyone took advantage of Germany's northern climate,
which was one of the softer experiences of those dog days of the
    ominous heatwave,
wildfires, droughts, floods, late June,
the Russian missiles hit a shopping centre in Kremenchuk,
with over a thousand people
browsing the sales racks,
tugging at a copper zipper in the fitting room,
picking up the yellow pacifier the baby threw out of the stroller,
pointing to a slice of poppyseed cake,
and, back home, Putin signed off to extend the 'gay-propaganda' law,
green light to intimidations, arrests, and sentencing
of anyone, adult or child,
caught with a thread
of homo-deemed content,
and, like our genetics,
(if I remember correctly from the only day of biology class
during which I didn't disassociate
to daydream about girls I was talking to online)
that, according to our DNA, mean any two human beings

picked on this earth at random
are 99.9 per cent
identical,
which, as I deduce, means
we basically all have
homo-deemed content
in us
(I was never good at science, but it seems like a fair comparison),
Nadyenka had a plan
to make use of those nine euros,
she drafted the route
and made sandwiches for the train,
dark bread with *molochnaya kolbaca* and a slice of Swiss cheese and
    her pickled onions,
and we woke up early to catch
the U-Bahn to the train north to Lübbenau,
there's a large inland delta from the Spree river,
in that town the folk gossip was something about pregnant women,
because the place was known for its pickles,
stands with barrels of pickles to choose from,
and palettes of artisanal ice cream at every corner
(I guess the folk story was about childbearing tastebuds or fertile
    blessings),
the reference was lost on Nadezhda,
as we weren't talking about how desperately
I wanted a child,
and how adamantly
she didn't,
on the train, she showed me photos
of the river, she told me we would go kayaking there,
on the train, she was scrolling
so I was scrolling, I checked
my inbox, there was an email
from a journalist
with a flowering introduction in praise of my work
and a query for an interview,
(despite my big talk, I didn't get such emails often,
so, when I did, it whisked me away into a daydream of a secure fiscal
    and artistic situation, in that utopia I lived off my writing, and
    these emails flowed aplenty,

so much so that I sighed and moaned, Not another,
and, How will I fit all these in with the book tour?
as in this suspension of reality I always had
a forthcoming book tour that would take up
all my time,
sigh, moan,
and how would I fit my consistent and well-paid
book deals
into such a schedule?
sigh, moan –
sometimes I added a speech that needed to be written
for the graduating class of some limelight university,
or, dream big,
a prize I was informed I would receive,
in all these scenarios
my ultimate pleasure
was to complain
and even resent
all the validation,
attention,
and praise),
Nadezhda encouraged me
to google the journalist
and it was clear that she was *tema*
(a shortcut Russian word we all used for spotting lezzies
– though it was just any woman who looked like
she was into women – so not just lez, *tema*
just means 'theme', it was my favourite
flagging term, 'cause unlike all the other
ones in the other
languages that I know,
it wasn't descriptive of a person,
like the Russian *goluboi* (blue boy, meaning gay man),
or *rozovaya* (pink girl, meaning gay woman), which belonged
    more
to those who hated us, there was
*gouine, goudou* (dyke in French),
even the old-school lesser-used
*sauvageonne* (a wild child, or a lesbian),
which were meant to be reclaimed,

but sounded stuffy and limited, okay
there was also *nash chelovek* in Russian
for queers in general,
meaning one of us – not bad,
but *tema* was neutral, just a subject
that could be anyone's gaze,
in fact, it wasn't about gazing at all, it was just
being
there
with everything else that was being
there),
the journalist had an *-ova* family name,
and light-brown hair laid neatly behind her ears,
and thin, translucent eyes,
and then Nadezhda spoke the phrase
that I knew would ruin our afternoon:
She looks like your type,

we spent the rest of the train ride
in silence then precisions came and went
as natural and undetectable to Nadya
as the rotation of the earth
through darkness and light, to me,
a gradual eclipse
of my nerves,
I saw the shade come and go
on Nadya's face,

we hurried to rent the kayak, Nadya insisting on a day like today
they would go fast,
ours would be ready in an hour's time,
and went to the riverside café for lunch in the meantime,
we ordered a beetroot and walnut salad and a club sandwich, the
    options
seemed strikingly out of place for the folky Germanic location
with quaint lakefront houses, a stone well in the garden each, and
    small wooden bridges edged with wild flowers,
but this must have been an indication of the type of tourists
they were hoping to attract (and it seems we fit the category),
I restrained myself until the server took our order,

then he turned his back
and I said,
Why don't you trust me,
and her face rotated into a gaunt evening,
despite the blaring sun on the terrace,

I do,
she said in a low voice, I would have
pulled out my hair,
or at least pulled on it,
if we weren't in public,
I tried
to use my words,
we went around in circles,
I cried,
eventually she said,
Don't cry,
please don't cry,
her voice amassed
my tears all the more,
toppling from my eyes, wet clothes
sliding off the balcony,
my gut clutching onto itself,
I was nauseous,
I didn't bring
my Xanax with me
and I was afraid this would turn
into a panic attack
as it often had
when we went around in circles
and I pulled at my hair,
I began to do my breathing technique
as discretely as I could, inhaling,
looking at my feet, blowing
the air out like a broken pipe,
she got up from her steel garden chair,
it scraped the cement,
I winced,
she kneeled down at my right
and put her hands on my knee,

she let me have the last pickle, turning the plate
in my direction, Because
I only want one thing in life,
she said,
to love you,

our kayak glided through the pale riverway
hued with clouds reflecting from above,
and the tangled vines and round-leaved bushes
mirrored on the bank,
upon which lily pads glazed and skitted on the ripples
our kayak made when it split the waters ahead of us in half,
Nadyenka was in the front
and I was in the back,
at first, she got angry at me
for paddling too slow,
but I told her,
Please speak to me gently
today, she excused herself,
but did it when her back
was facing me, she did speak gently
afterwards, I hurried
up my paddling, we found our rhythm
and slid forward,
the birds chirped,
the branches rustled,
and the ducks quacked and parted ways, Nadyenka turned around
    in her seat
and looked back at me,
I smiled shyly,
she told me,
I trust you,
I'm not sure
that I believed her, but I wanted
to kiss her, I tilted
forward, the shift was bigger
than I thought, I was afraid the boat
would flip over, I tilted back and continued
to paddle,

the summer
before Nadezhda and I met, my mother was healthy, my mama
    and I
were planning a trip together
back to Ukraine,
it would be my first time back since I left
when it was still part of the Soviet Union, I was anxious
about seeing my mama
and seeing my birth city, then Kharkov,
now Kharkiv,
and what a stranger I would be
to both,
my mama didn't help,
telling me that, when we're there, I'd have to watch
my back at all times, Ukraine is a dangerous place
and Kharkiv a dangerous city, it's no
America, she chuckled,
though years back she and my father
had been held up at gun-point
on one of their evening walks,
they didn't have anything on them
except house keys
and toffee candies my mom liked to suck on
for her asthma, It's dangerous
in a different way, Mama explained, always explaining
the world to me,
a world she herself deemed
unexplainable,
There are two systems, my mother expanded upon her statement,
    the visible one and the invisible one,
and in the West you are used to the visible one,
but in the East you have to attune yourself to the invisible one,
but don't worry, my friend Shurka will take us around in her car,
we, of course, shouldn't go anywhere by foot,
and she's got the necessary friends
if we run into trouble, Shurka
had also helped me with my birth certificate
a couple years prior
when I was applying for my French nationality,

my original one was Soviet,
handwritten,
wherein my nationality was 'Jewish',
and the French government couldn't accept paperwork from a
    country
and nationality
that didn't exist,
technically I had to go back to Kharkiv
to confirm my birth in the registry there
and re-do my paperwork,
it would have taken a while,
not to mention I was still nerve-wrecked and not ready
to go back to Ukraine,
free Ukraine,
my beloved Ukraine,
that didn't bat
an eyelash
when nearly 300,000
Ukrainian Jews
left
their home,
Shurka
smoothed everything over (we sent her money) and I received my
    new
Ukrainian birth certificate, I held
the thick paper in my hands, maybe
now I would let myself
be loved,

I told you Shurka would sort it, Mama said,
You have to know, she explained, that you can't trust
a Slav, but
you can always rely on them,

when my mama and I began talking about
the trip back, I started researching
queer life in Ukraine,
to see what was up
since the grim homogeneity of the Soviet era,
the first fruits of my labour

were bleak, a reminder that search engines bear witness
to the foulness upon which
a civilisation can thrive, Ukrainian police
listed fourteen
recorded hate crimes against gender identity and orientation that
    year,
but human rights organisations listed the number
closer
to 140,
most being unreported, underground
far-right organisations kept better track
of their targets than
police of the
victims, hate groups have a knack
for organising, they gathered and
published names, addresses, phones numbers, photos of queer
    activists,
and sent text messages around their dark web community,
police deemed them
untraceable, one of Nadya's friends, Ksenia,
a boyish blonde with a cowlick
and wrist tattoos, she always had a muscle-grip
on whatever she was carrying,
a coffee mug, her mobile phone, another girl's hand,
she had immigrated to Berlin when the Russians invaded,
she had been part of the LBGT+ activist groups there, helped
organise Kyiv Pride,
she told us how much she loved Kyiv,
her friends,
her country,
but
she received photographs of her balcony and the entrance to her
    building,
the last message she got
before she decided to leave
was a short SMS that read,
*You're next,*
we tried
to upkeep our coffee dates with Ksenia,
Nadya said she was a nice girl, but

everything's about activism with her,
I argued that it's thanks to people like her
that we have what that we have,
that we are
free,
but I secretly
agreed, she was a bit of a broken record,
I didn't care, though, I had a Cossack sort of sorority
with any and every Ukrainian, Ksenia
met a German girl two months in, Lotte,
who was a suave dyke,
oily dark hair
hanging over her collarbone,
biker boots,
James Dean Levi's,
that kind of girl,
who was meant to always be
someone's girlfriend,
and she had an overlapping way of dating,
went from a two-year thing
straight to dating Ksenia,
which is what it is,
I like to stay out of it,
only because deeming others' relationships as failures
is an awful habit I'm trying to break, before
Ksenia arrived
a distant friend in London, Artur,
who kept up with things,
had been collecting funds for queer organisations in Saint Pete,
the city they had left seven years prior,
to be able to do things,
like collect funds for queer organisations back home,
and stay alive,
Artur wanted to be
the person that they were,
a non-binary trans person,
Artur had vigour,
a newly fleeced chin,
rosy cheeks,
and resolute green eyes with a paradoxical spark,

reserved and outspoken,
Arturchik, how they raged for Yelena Grigoryeva
before and after the fact, she was
a queer activist and organisation leader in Saint Pete,
she had flagged Russian gay-hunting groups who created 'kill sites'
with lists containing
personal information
and rewards
for the execution of queer people,
a list she herself
was on, she went to the Saint Pete law enforcement,
but hunting games are just
games,
hunting
white horses,
horseplay,
three days later,
Yelena Grigoryeva,
was found in a bush near her home,
with multiple stab wounds
and strangulation bruises, the last photo
she posted on her social media
was of her in the Saint Petersburg streets
holding a sign,
declaring her undaunted support
for three Russian teenage sisters
who had killed their father
after years of sexual torture, love
is not blind, the law
is blind, the grains of sand are rushing
down the tight glass throat
of time,
in Grigoryeva's last week,
she asked her friend to take good care of her cat
in the event of her death, her funeral
was tense, friends who gathered
eyed building windows,
checked under their cars,
the prize money for Grigoryeva's death
could be doubled

if the executioner also
attended her burial,
Arturchik
tattooed her initials
in the centre of their chest,
between the two scars
from their top surgery,

our kayak glided through the pale riverway
hued with clouds reflecting from above,
and we,
two Soviet kids
not knowing how to kiss
without capsizing,
hued with the trembling of water
reflecting from below,

there was a Soviet short animation film, made in the '70s,
Soviet stop-motion was breathtaking
between folk and art brut,
the sketch strokes, the way the faces
changed with a couple bends
of a pen line,
and the clay figures,
bendy embroidery
and shapeshifting clumps of life with the chimes and strings of the
        soundscapes,
and the characters,
animals
or clocks
or witches
were all philosophers,
leaving us with more wilderness
than we could house within, they were visual meditations
unknown to the world as we know it
even for nine minutes, Nadyenka loved
animals and I loved
animals, she said, I'm the hedgehog
in that animation film, do you know it? I didn't know it,
she showed me it, *Yozhik v Tumane*,

The Hedgehog in the Fog, it's evening,
and every evening the hedgehog (Yozhik) and his friend the bear
    cub (Medvezhonok) meet to have tea and count the stars,
Yozhik steps out of his house to meet Medvezhonok
with a special treat, a jar of raspberry jam, but this evening
the air is murky, something's
not right, Yozhik
walks down the path, and the fog
thickens around him, and we see
that there is a creature shadowing him, a suspicious owl with deep-
    set eyes,
and the fog is thickening
and the owl disappears, his path
takes him through the woods and there
a beautiful white horse, Yozhik stops,
exalted by the stallion,
but the fog is thickening,
and the white horse is blanketed and erased, he hears
a voice calling out to him,
Yozhiiiik, Yoooozzzhiiik,
he hurries up and now he's in the valley
Yozhiiiik, Yoooozzzhiiik,
he hurries up,
but the fog is thickening, and Yozhik is no longer sure of his way,
he blinks and blinks
and all of a sudden there is a glimmer of the white horse
and he stumbles towards the sight,
but at his feet there is just a snail riding a floating leaf, he reaches down
towards the snail, but it floats away into the white vapour,
Yozhiiiik, Yoooozzzhiiik,
the outline of an elephant surfaces and Yozhik is startled,
he twists and gropes for a new path, the fog
is thickening and the elephant disappears, the shadow
of a black bat flaps forth, Yozhik jumps and turns, he sees
a glimmer
of the white horse again,
how sublime a creature lives with us on this earth,
Yozhiiiik, Yoooozzzhiiik,
he hurries, runs, trips, tumbles, through the thickening fog,
the special jar of jam rolls out of his hand,

Yozhiiiik, Yoooozzzhiiik,
he pats around for the jar, he can't
come to his friend's house empty-handed,
he grabs the glass pot, only to fall into a river,
jar tight to his chest, Yozhik decides to give himself over
to the river, let it take me
where it wants to take me, the fog is thick as skin,
he sees nothing,
Yozhiiiik, Yoooozzzhiiik,
I'll go where I go, a fish swims up to his side,
she pulls him to shore, where the fog
is thinning, and he sees
the woods, the valley, and the road
to his friend's house, he takes it
and arrives at Medvezhonok's doorstep, his dear friend has been
    worried about Yozhik,
the *samovar* is losing its heat,
and the juniper twigs in the fire have nearly turned to ash,
but Medvezhonok moves two wicker chairs out onto the porch, he
    tells Yozhik
there is no one else with whom he'd rather count the stars,
they sit side by side and drink their tepid tea, Medvezhonok
begins to count,
but Yozhik's lost in the sky above,
he notes the stars with his friend,
but keeps on thinking
about that white horse,

Arturchik
was full of data, and it emboldened them,
such numbers overwhelm me,
they do not make me brave,
perhaps I responded less and less
to their texts
because I was afraid they'd sniff out a coward
from my trail, and one evening
I was crying my eyes out again,
but it was also a last-straw type of crying,
Nadezhda
had said something to upset me

then said something to comfort me,
I was unravelling, I kept repeating
I'm not strong enough for this,
Nadya took a tone,
This relationship? Me?
I had snot on my upper lip,
Nadyenka leaned back then got up then paced
in the living room
with nowhere to go, I'm not strong enough
to live,
I guess I was a broken record too,
but there were so many moments
where I felt my own courage,
aside from showmanship,
maybe not courage,
but peace,
maybe not peace,
but majesty,
the fine hairs on Nadyenka's forearm,
the cats on the roof
who flashed their neon eyes at us
in the dark,
one of the last texts I got from Arturchik
was something about a long-term visa they secured and
a data point, I think,
they said, it's no surprise but
that a survey was done and
nearly one out of every five Russians
agreed
that we should eliminate
gay and lesbian and trans people from society,

(with my own relentless depression, the irony was not lost on me,
the shadowboxing that stretched the length of our lives,
wanting so badly
at times
to die
and fighting so hard
at times
to not be killed)

Nadyenka and I spent most of March in Berlin, we were being horribly
kissy-kissy
in the street,
and it seemed the Berliners were being uptight
(I was used to the Paris way, there were always couples
making out hardcore
while one was caressing the back pockets of the other's jeans,
and yet, in that same Paris, dare you step outside the dress code
or performance
of your allotted and perceived
gender,
the whole city huffed and puffed,
while in Berlin, anything goes,
really, express yourself,
but no sloppy
public intimacy
*bitte* and *danke*,
in Paris, we felt like rebels,
in Berlin, we felt like rebels),
we turned on Böhmischer Platz
towards the Vietnamese place we liked,
and then I stalled again,
my cheek turning over her shoulder,
away from her,
to the grey Skoda at the red light, sure it
looked like Pasha in the passenger seat,
it could have been him,
if he hadn't done something so stupid
that I for years
had wanted to do,
the guy unbuckled his seat belt
and rebuckled it,
it was chaffing his shoulder I think,
it was keeping him
on earth,

the law called it *muzhelozhstvo*,
meaning men lying together,
so all that gay stuff
had been illegal

since the early nineteenth century,
but then the Bolsheviks threw their coup
and got to the nucleus of the Russian Imperialist membrane,
1917, they cleaned the slate of the old penal code,
and it seemed that a new Russia had risen,
but as soon the new Soviet government got what's what
(fatherless Yasha),
Stalin reinstalled the law against *muzhelozhstvo*,
it was up to five years in Siberia for the gay stuff,
or someone ratting you out
for doing gay stuff, which
may have been gay
or not,
just to save their own skin,
in Siberia you'd be set to work on the frozen tundra
felling timber, laying railroads, constructing canals,
or the special task
of mining uranium in the secret raw-material facilities
(like the Tabosharsky region of Tadjikistan)
where atomic weaponry was being hush-hush developed,
the prisoners paying their dues to their country
by sweeping the floors of the test sites,
decontaminating the area,
without so little as a face mask, glove,
or, at times, a fully soled shoe, there weren't
any laws against 'women lying together'
since the very idea of such an act
was considered unachievable,
except in artwork
and mythology, but really
it's because male subversion was dangerous to the law,
and female subversion was dangerous to nature,
still women loving women,
though untermed, did not go unpunished,
their gulags were sanitariums and mental asylums
where their behaviour was
diagnosed as a disease, separate
from their being, and thus curable,
(though the cure did involve
clinically killing off the being

carrying the disease),
whereas gay men were just generally
gay all over, but by the '60s
it wasn't only the queers
who wanted sexual freedom, skip ahead
and Yeltsin's government had repealed the sodomy laws in 1993,
bars, discos, hubs for anyone who was *nash chelovek* —
well, I wouldn't say sprang up,
but cautiously emerged within discrete exteriors,
or within cipher loitering,
subtextuals rather than homosexuals,
like in the city centre of Moscow,
the Bolshoi Theatre's stately white pillars gleamed in the
    approaching dusk,
holding up the statue of a four-steed horseman, mid-fury ahead,
the quadriga of Apollo, Apollo's chariot, galloping
across the heavens on his golden flames
bringing daylight
to the world,
the afternoon's rain left a rosy dew on the stone,
and a wet fog was thickening
from the foaming fountain in front,
around which men walked,
eying each other, the *pleshka*,
Russian slang for such pick-up spots
(the term, a bald spot on top of a man's head,
the reference,
perhaps on the cruiser's circling trail
or their alluded advanced age), if life
doesn't give you anything
it will at least leave you
with irony, and so,
this Neoclassical triumph of Russian muscle and ideal,
wherein, on 30th December 1922, the Bolshevik revolutions pro-
    claimed the existence
of a new country, the USSR,
the national glory that graces the 100-ruble banknote,
stands cheek to cheek with the exaltation of faggot geometry,
amidst the historical monuments and boulevards,
near Kitay-gorod metro or Gogolevsky Boulevard, and elsewhere,

the god Apollo
could supposedly see into the future,

what did he see while bringing dawn to the faces
of men,
fine-grained, sleep-lined,
broad-collared, bearded,
buzz-cut and cherub-curled,
Muscovites and farm boys,
military men and intellectuals,
polished leather shoes or worn hide, fraying laces,
turning evening into night in the fountain fog,

we got a corner spot at the Vietnamese place, and the temperature
    began drastically dropping,
the owner closed the door firmly, clipping off the draught, Nadyenka
translated the menu for me, patching together
English and Russian words
to describe the Vietnamese ingredients written in German,
I know what you'll get, Nadyenka said,
because they do it best here, I rarely
ate red meat,
and Nadyenka often,
but it smelled good,
and looked even better, she ordered two
beef bo buns
for us, I told you so, Nadyenka said,
who insisted that her dreams were informing the events to come,
like Dasik, who was trying to tell her that her ex-wife would lie
so terribly it would not be something
she would be able to see
with her eyes, The dream told me so, Nadyenka maintained
as she maintained
what I would order, because she also maintained
that she could see
into the future,

Nadya's father
took out a loan for her to go to a beauty institute
about which she had been talking his ear off, her passion

had been not so much cosmetics as
human skin cells and hair follicles, her parents
were never much interested in stories, literary or otherwise,
they were the plain-dealing kind,
her mother had always stayed at home and taken care of Nadya
(housewives, a rarity in Soviet society),
and her father's profession in the Soviet Union was ambiguous to
    Nadyenka,
and even less clear to me,
some specialised handiwork
for the criminal police,
which I couldn't quite imagine when I met him,
he was buff, okay,
but awfully hesitant,
and he stuttered and flustered easily, Nadya said he never went into
    specifics,
he took his family and got out of Moscow
for a new life, explicitly and implicitly, it wasn't
a story he had told Nadya directly,
more of a self-speech emitted in post-work fatigue,
back in the day he had a buddy, an investigator or detective,
    something like this,
when he'd see his buddy, his buddy would get more and more
nervous, dart-eyed, he swallowed his saliva a lot,
at the time, his buddy had a wife and son a couple years younger
    than Nadyenka,
maybe five years old,
there was a week his buddy's eyes were laced with red veins,
he asked him if he was getting enough sleep,
he had to fill the space between them with some words
that were neither too doubtful
nor too certain,
he had chosen those, even though he knew they were stupid,
everyone knew
what eyes like that meant, then his work buddy just
stopped coming to work, He was my friend, he had mumbled out
    loud,
a real genuine guy, the thing is
I really liked him,
and he really liked me, not three weeks after

he heard his buddy's little boy
got abducted, Nadya's father
had lots of questions of course,
but if someone's kid got abducted,
it wasn't an accident, it was a message,
and Nadya's mama told his father, For God's sake stay out of it,
his buddy was an investigator or detective, after all,
so word is he investigated and detected
and eventually he just received an anonymous note
with the exact location of where
his little boy's body
could be found
in case he wanted to bury him,

in Berlin, he's a mechanic,
and a football fan,
and otherwise likes cars and car parts,
and to work and to tell his wife and Nadyenka
how much he works,
he works a lot,
and his wife leaves the TV on, switching back and forth between
    Russian channels,
while she tries out recipes in the kitchen, the books
Nadya had in the house growing up
were not many,
but there were two thick volumes,
medical books (every Slavic family had medical books, we were
our own doctors), I never took interest
in the ones hanging out on my family's shelves, Nadya did,
those were the books
that swept Nadyenka away
from the stiff apartment
and the unpredictable moods of her mother
and car-raptured father,

Nadya has a habit
of grabbing pill boxes out of my hands
to read the ingredients
and explain their chemistry to me, I, thankfully,
don't have an addictive personality,

at least not to medication, which is great
because I have a lot
of medication
at my disposal, I really do
try my best
to only take what I need, but it's hard
to know what you need
when you're not on the right
medication,
Nadya told me that she often wishes she would have gone into
    cosmetic
surgery,
all those veins and nerves, and the minutiae of creation,
and it pays well, and we both would have liked very much
to be rich, Oh well, Nadyenka likes what she does, she even has
a couple of very rich clients from Russia on the side,
*nouveau richniki,* and when they're in Berlin
she does her signature face massage
(that surrogate-Botox technique
that plumps and firms and pulls
the skin and takes off a good handful
of years, but lasts around twenty-four hours,
nature is nature,
it was a little something you could get
before a night out
or photo shoot), after the massage,
she does their hair and make-up,
it's a lot of Instagram-look requests,
smoky eyes and contouring and all that,
easy cash, except for
the small talk, though if anyone was good at chit-chatting through
    worlds
it was Nadezhda,
but there were evenings
when she came home from one of these appointments,
an envelope of cash in hand,
exhausted, and not just physically,
which could be remedied with rest,
but spiritually, for which I gave as generously as I could
my undivided presence of mind and heart, she asked me

if she could bury
her head
between my bicep and ribcage, she told me she doesn't want to cry
    about it,
but it's like you keep so much bitterness about
all those things that were taken away from you,
only to realise
you, yourself,
gave them away,

neither Nadya or I fit into the old-school *pasivnaia/aktivnaia* dynamic,
passive/active, femme/butch,
we're both dykes who would have loved
to live
in 1930s or 1980s Berlin,
the slick hair, finger-curl Dietrich tailoring,
new-wave dark brows and blue eyeshadow coloured in from lash
    to eyebrow,
the tough underground femme, East/West graffiti,
the dandy femme, the lezzie Mata Hari,
*banditka*, street-kid, thug-prophet,
deconstructionist comrade, I told her I was non-binary,
and she said, Me too, but for her
it's more of a private feeling,
maybe I had something to prove, I insisted on the 'she/they',
but felt cramped when referred to as 'she'
and cramped when referred to as 'they',
sometimes I think I can only know myself
through what I have
to push against, I don't want
to be known, I've also been heard proclaiming,
I was having a little fit
with myself, it was before summer, I don't want
anyone
to see me anymore, I banged
my fist on the desk in my Paris apartment, and the cheap thing almost
    cracked a leg,
it was highly unsatisfying,
I would have preferred to bang the wall,
not for the anger but for

the physical pain, but I had worked
so hard
with my therapist
to quit that self-harm thing, I just took
a step back and stood close
to my bed and raised my hands above my head and threw punches
    and growled shamelessly
at the emptiness around me, I've always been
a fighter, but struggled
to choose the right cause,


Nadya emphasised that she had close friends
that were Jews,
and even dated an older Jewish woman for a couple of months
(Nadya told me that she had earnestly thought she could fall in love
    with her, but turns out she was just deeply attracted
to her way of mourning, the woman's wife
had died of a kidney disease
she later discovered was hereditary, a year and half before she had
    met Nadya),
I like Jews,
Nadezhda said with such pride
that I couldn't help but recognise
the generations of Soviets
who twirled upon their blind eye, she
didn't have to understand, I decided, I wanted her to understand
that she didn't understand,


there's so much
to not understand,


an influential work
on the twentieth-century Russian conception of gender
was written by the young Viennese Otto Weininger,
called *Sex and Character*,
published one month after his twenty-third birthday, within a year's
    time

it would become a hit in Austro-Hungary,
and his quill would later influence writers from Ludwig Wittgenstein
    to James Joyce,
but five months after the publication Weininger
shot himself
in the rented house where Beethoven (his favourite composer)
    lived
and died,
he was, as many published males of his time, 'a genius'
(and misogynist and anti-Semite, despite being a Jew himself),
I won't say yay or nay on the quality of this thought,
but he did have a telling chapter that boils down to
Jewishness and femaleness sharing two essential aspects: their
    uncontrolled desire and that they both
possessed the unreliable effeminate qualities of moodiness, trickery,
    and hysteria,
August Strindberg and the Nazi party were big fans of the book
(though the regime did simultaneously condemn the Jew-author),
but you can't hate yourself without someone else
hating you,
Freud
explained
Weininger's mental health and suicide was just
the castration complex
– something that all Jews
and women shared,


there's this joke and it goes like this:
it's a hot day,
and there are three women eating ice cream,
one is licking the vanilla scoop,
the second is sucking on the vanilla scoop,
and the third is biting at the vanilla scoop, which one
of them is a lesbian?


. . . the woman who owns the ice cream shop.


Yuri arrived in Moscow in the mid-'90s,
just as the first gay clubs were opening up, like

Tri Obez'yany (Three Monkeys), Khameleon (Chameleon) and
    Chance,
they weren't flashy-homo
just places where people who knew
knew, and those who didn't
sometimes stopped by and got a feeling
then went to the bar and ordered a drink and by the time their
    drink came
they clocked that the men were awfully close with one another,
and the women eyed each other with appetite,
and then put two and two together
and shuffled out in a hurry
before anyone thought they were
one of us, Yuri
was from a farm in Siberia, he had a thing for clothes,
and he was always dressed to the nines, a slope-cheeked dandy
with a pencil-thin moustache
and flared-trousers, he was a budding womenswear designer, his
    brother
tried to kill him when he was sixteen
for looking at Western women's magazines, Yuri didn't tell us,
it was whispered to me at one of those dinners
I didn't want to go to, but I went
with Nadya, she did my hair and I loved that,
she put a finger-curl that framed my face, and parted hers in the
    middle
and slicked it back as taut as night, and we both wore
oversized blazers,
Nadyenka kept shouting out the time, and we took turns
looking up the weather
and debating whether or not it would rain, Nadyenka liked
biking in the rain, I got sick easily
and just being out in the rain, even if I was wrapped up and under
    an umbrella
would send me home with a cough,
that would turn into a sneeze,
that would flare up my sinusitis
or turn to strep throat overnight,
we decided to the leave the bikes, and took the U-Bahn towards
    Friedrichshain,

but I replayed the evening's decision
as I looked out the scratched-up window of the train
into the darkness of the tunnel
that neither reflected nor absorbed my face,
I still felt it
glued to my skull,
it worried me
that Nadyenka hadn't initially proposed we take the train
when she saw the seventy per cent chance of rain,
knowing of my feeble health,
and that she kept presenting arguments in favour of taking the bikes
before finally handing the ruling over to me
with a tepid As you wish, I chewed it over,
my psyche was chattering, the devil is in the details,
and there was a devil, your woman
cared more about her bike ride
than you, granted
I didn't always trust my brain
but I had made a promise to myself,
that I would trust
my brain, but also trust
the woman I trust,

we arrived and the apartment was warmly lit,
a cobalt-glazed ceramic vase holding powder-rose peonies
on the glass entry table, Yurchik
kissed us on the cheek and his husband that he had met in Moscow
    and moved back to Berlin with him in the early 2000s, Jonas,
yelled out from the hallway that he's sorry if the place smells like
    garlic (it did), Jonas was turning fifty
and he had told Yuri, On my birthday, you'll be kissing
a dragon,
I knew Yuri very little, and Jonas even less, it was Nadya that had
    met Jonas during those years I wasn't a part of,
he had also been back and forth from Moscow, like Nadyenka, but
    they always missed each other in that city, the others
were already there (I still couldn't get used to the German punctuality,
    we were
always running late, and I gladly took the blame, one of the
    Parisian traits I held onto preciously,

whatever country I was in, I know it's disrespectful,
but it's the same reason why I kept repeating certain grammatical
    mistakes
in French, switching the direct and indirect object for example,
saying *Je l'ai donné* instead of *Je lui ai donné* on purpose,
and in Russian, hanging onto my awkward formal vocabulary,
saying *prekrasno*, wonderful, instead of *kruto*, cool,
and stuffing my English with outdated idioms,
the thing is,
I never had a language that I could truly call
my native language,
after kindergarten we left Soviet Ukraine,
I never did any more schooling in Russian,
and then it was a quick-paced race of my ABCs in the US of A,
and then it was proving that my history didn't own me,
and my will was stronger than national red tape,
if I wanted to be French, I would be French
– and as soon as I became French,
I found the language and culture
hypocritical and irritating –
but in every apprenticeship of identity
I was calling out
to my beloved language,
Take me,
I'm yours!
I wasn't anybody's, and I wouldn't
be taken, I was begging
lexicon and grammar,
while deforming it, gritting,
if those words wouldn't accept me,
then I wouldn't accept them, I pledged
not to love
a single word
I couldn't pervert),

Nadyenka didn't allot the same dignity
to my perpetual tardiness, she listened
but told me to try
and (pretty please) get my shit together
'cause it was really rude,

Yuri took our coats and we scurried to the dinner table and did our
    round of introductions,
her name was Alla, she sat to my left,
she was about Yuri and Jonas's age, wore a tight-fitting purple
    sweater and her blonde hair piled on her head twisted like a
    lemon, she was curvy
and liked it, and she kept filling me in
on all sorts of details, she had met Yurchik in Moscow, he still has
    the scars,
his brother said he only regretted
that the knife didn't do the trick, said he'd do it again
if he had the chance, 'cause
he'd rather have a brother in the grave
than a faggot,
his brother ended up
dying young
in a car accident
is what Yuri heard, he hadn't seen him since he left for the big
    city,
and then Alla refilled her glass with the dark-amber Georgian wine
    she had brought,
made from a Rkatsiteli grape, she informed me as she poured,
she had a fling, she told me later in the night, with a well-built dyke
    from Tbilisi
(Alla likes shoulders and a solid jaw),
she made it seem like it was one eternal night and a never-reaching
    dawn,
but then it was clear it had lasted for years,
and a drop of wine was rolling off the rim of her glass
as she gravitated the bottle over mine and poured it full, though I
    didn't
ask for any, I drank it anyways,
Alla was a time-honoured femme, she had the mannerisms
of a big boss's woman, and there was something titillating
about a woman who moved as if
she let men fuck her
but knowing there were only the powerhouse hands
of a dyke
that went between her legs, I'm not sure if it aroused me
because I still had that Slavic male gaze

to deconstruct, but it sure made my mouth,
and other things,
water,
the vixen, the tease, the dictator's flame,
Nadyenka was these things, but darker,
a femme of the shadows,
and I loved that,
the way she moved, fatal, spy-like,
and the way she grabbed me all over
like a mafioso, I guess both of us
got very horny
at that romanticised fascist role-play, I didn't want
to sleep with Alla or anything,
but Nadyenka noticed the way
Alla (who, to be fair, was a coquette to everyone) chit-chatted only
to her right, where I happened
to be sitting, I wouldn't say
she gave me any extra attention beside the fact that
the person sitting to her left
was lovey-dovey for his boyfriend across the table,
and she had no one else to talk to,
I tried to explain to Nadyenka
on the train back,
I was way too soft a dyke to be attractive to Alla, I didn't have any
    macho
(first- or second-degree)
in me, that I was clearly not
Alla's type,
But she is yours, Nadya said,
I paused,
It was so obvious, Nadyenka was raising her voice, describing how
my empty wine glass
became full,
Nadyenka was bellowing,
I became aware
that we might be
making a scene, the skin on my face
started to tingle, Nadyenka howled
and I stayed
very silent,

Nadyenka's mama keeps her and her father's apartment methodically
      clean, as she did,
when Nadya was young, and lived with them,
Nadya keeps our apartment methodically clean, not just the
      apartment,
but her clothes, her shoes, her plant-life, no dust, no lint, no stains,
never, never,
she says she had a lot of toys as a child thanks to her aunt,
Nadyenka's father's sister, who had access to Western products,
and money, she was the first of the family to move
to Europe,
when Nadyenka was thirteen she got a pair of white sneakers from
      her, they glowed
and Nadya put on the sneakers with white socks and a jean skirt,
      You have such
beautiful legs, her mama let out, a ballerina,
her mama never had much to talk about,
but back then she could go on and on about
how beautiful her daughter was,
with her snow-princess features, valley-blue eyes, dark-river hair,
      that year
it rained sporadically, though the temperature gave them a warm
      spring, it was the first day
Nadyenka wore her shoes to school,
white socks, and her jean skirt,
after school
she didn't want to go home right away, she felt so
beautiful, in her new shoes, white socks, jean skirt, she took the bus
around the city a bit, stopped by a cosmetics shop,
took the long way, and then
the fog began to thicken, the air
was damp, and thunder broke through the sky, then the rainfall
all at once, Nadyenka ran and ran
through the curtains
of water, it was already dark,
she couldn't miss curfew, she entered
the apartment, her mother
was waiting for her, Nadya was soaked
from head to toe, and her white sneakers
now mushy and yellowed,

her mother told her to take off her wet shoes,
Nadya took off the spongy shoes and then the socks, and her
    mother told her,
Get undressed,
and Nadyenka peeled off the layers until she was in her pre-teen
    bra and underwear,
and then her mother picked up the mud-stuck, dripping shoes, one
    in each hand,
and smacked Nadya in the face with the right one,
then she went to the kitchen
and threw the sneakers
into the trash,

before school the next day,
Nadyenka went out discretely and picked through the dumpster but
    she couldn't find them,
Nadya told me this story without flinching,
another aspect that worried me, what would happen,
if I revealed to her
how much pain she was in, her mother's father
was a total alcoholic
and played knock out with the kids
(that's how the story always goes), I was asking how
her father could let her mother
treat her this way, what did he do
about it,
Nothing, Nadya said,
men do nothing,

my papa
would tear a person's limbs off
before he let them touch me,
but then there's the psychological – I had everything as a child,
Nadya summarised, my aunt sent me a whole collection of stuffed
    animals, I lined them up in my room, and I would sit for hours
    and play with them
(Nadyenka was a wallflower kid, lost in her own thoughts, her
    mother often had to yell
her name many times
to snap her out of it),

*Naddyaaaa, Naddddyyyyaaaaaaaaaaaa,*
when she was playing, and her mama would come into her room,
Nadya never knew if she was going to hug her
or hit her,

Men do nothing,
Nadyenka said, until
they do something,

things weren't going well and it's nothing new,
men like to drink (maybe that's what saved my father,
his father was a brutal alcoholic too, and he vowed to stay away
    from liquor,
and he did,
the last time he drank was a glass of champagne at my brother's
    wedding),
I don't want to say liquor
turns men bad,
but it certainly doesn't
turn them good,
the generations come and go,
and the lessons don't stick, Nadya
was a good student, but laboured
with maths, got low grades,
which was inadmissible in a Russian household, her father
being quick with numbers
began to go over her algebra homework with her after work,
which coincided with when her father began to drink heavily, after
    work,
she couldn't solve for x, it really irritated her old man, 'cause
it wasn't that hard,
to solve for x, yet she couldn't
do it, her old man
grabbed the binder from her hands
and knocked her over the head with it,
he never did that kind of thing when she was young,
she doesn't know why
it started with the maths homework, and then it was
her mother that comforted her,
confusing role switch, her mama

put the frozen *pelmeni* bag (Russian dumplings)
on her forehead,

like me, Nadya also has
panic attacks, but they generally come
from logistical mistakes,
a missed train, a wrong document, a faulty receipt,
her reaction is so extreme
that it took me a couple of months to understand
that she was not exaggerating
or acting out with an ulterior motive,
but having a very real breach of reality,
*Kakaya durochka!* she would start muttering,
What an idiot! sometimes I had to grab her wrists
'cause she did this thing
where it looked like she wanted
to split her skull in half,
it's hard to explain, but even harder
to convince her that she's not stupid,
why would she be stupid,
for standing on the wrong platform? I might as well,
she said under her breath,
have jumped onto the rails,

Nadya always put her mama on speaker phone,
perhaps to have a witness,
You were, her mama said with the softness of yogurt,
a beautiful daughter,
we both understood why
she used the past tense,
I was, Nadyenka told me after she hung up,
a beautiful baby, I mean really
beautiful, people noticed me
in the stroller, You are,
I told her, a beautiful woman,
Didn't you hear it in her voice? Nadyenka said,
I've let myself go, and I'm
a cow now,
in my head ran thoughts
I knew not to say out loud, like

that cows are beautiful creatures,
I like cows,
perhaps the way that Nadyenka
likes Jews,
I'm glad I said other things,
the things you say
to the woman you love,
a good refrain
can save a life, You are
beautiful, I tell you,
and you are
free,


a merchant had a beautiful daughter whose name was Vasilisa,
her mother was dying
when she was turning
eight, she gave Vasilisa
a tiny wooden doll with the instructions to never
ever
tell anyone of this doll, not even
her father,
the doll would help her
when she needed help, her mother died,
Vasilisa gripped the doll
to her hip, blank-eyed,
the doll pulled from her
the pain
that squeezed
the girl, the grief
eased up, the months
turned into years, her father
found a new woman, a widow
with two daughters from her previous marriage, he explained to
    Vasilisa
that it's no good for a girl
to grow up
motherless,
then he left to the seas on business, Vasilisa's step-mother (you
    guessed it)
was cruel, she couldn't stand the sight of Vasilisa

because (you guessed it) she was beautiful and pure
and her daughters were (you guessed it) grisly and dinged, she
    forced
Vasilisa to do household tasks
day and night,
then cleaned her up to show off in town
to attract men, and then lure these men
over to her daughters, her step-sisters
complained to their mother that she was being too soft
on the gross girl, the mother said, Be my guest,
and the step-sisters used their imagination
to educate Vasilisa in the waste of space that she was, using tactics
that later advanced civilisations would include as part of their
    playbook
for torture, like
the rat technique where
you tie the prisoner to a table, put a rat on their chest, put a steel
    bucket on the rat, and make a low fire on top of the steel bucket,
    so that the rat begins to panic,
and, since it cannot burrow through steel, the scared vermin
burrows through your flesh,
things like this,
Vasilisa bloody, open-wounded, but still beautiful,
every night, her doll would heal her,
her father, the merchant, came and went,
noticing
nothing,
doing
nothing,
he was off on a long
business trip, the women moved house to a spot on the edge of the
    forest,
wherein the witch Baba Yaga was rumoured to live
(the land around was gloomy and barren,
but the family was most likely catching wind of a real estate
    investment in an area that would surely be gentrified),
it was now or never, the step-sisters tugged on their mother's arms,
    they had a plan,
one night they put out all the light in the household,
fireplace, candles, until it was pitch black

and the step-mother woke Vasilisa and told her to go into the forest
to get light from Baba Yaga's hut
(she was known to have light to spare, I guess,
I missed this part of the story), Vasilisa wrapped her doll
close to her chest and set out, the blackness
was thickening,
Vasiliiiisa, Vasssiiiiliiisaaa,
the wooden doll guided her step,
her feet sunk in the marshy earth then pulled back up
and sunk again, the sooty fog
was thickening, somewhere in that
airy muck, she spotted
a cavalier
all in white
riding a white horse, Vasilisa stopped,
she gazed
at the sublime creature, in awe of the steed,
Vasiliiiisa, Vasssiiiiliiisaaa,
the doll beckoned,
another cavalier dressed all in red
rode by on a red horse,
Vasiliiiisa, Vasssiiiiliiisaaa,
this one left her with a bad feeling, she quickly
pulled away,
her wooden doll eased her step,
forward, forward, then Stop,
the doll whispered,
and blackness thinned
and gave sight
to a fence made of skulls on wooden spires, behind which
stood a hut
on chicken legs,
We're here, the doll whispered,
Vasilisa got the gist, the eye sockets in the skulls lit up
like lanterns and out stepped
Baba Yaga
cloaked in her worn linen cape so that her face was
just shadow, Baba Yaga told her that if she wants light,
she's got to earn it,
and if she fails,

she'll be killed,

typical,

Vasilisa had no choice, she agreed

and Baba Yaga started her off with household chores,

she brushed the yard of pebbles and weeds, washed Baba Yaga's
    laundry in her big wooden bucket, separated poppyseeds from
    grains of soil, and so on,

Vasiliiiisa, Vasssiiiiliiiisaaa,

Don't despair, the doll breathed,

every night she massaged Vasilisa's blistered hands,

and wiped her salty tears,

then the next day it would start all over again,

Vasilisa picked out the rotten corn from the bowl on her infected
    knees,

swollen with mud, and the blackness began to thin, she looked up
and saw

the white horseman, What is it? she asked the doll,

It's the light of day, the doll answered,

and then she saw

a red horseman, What is it? she asked the doll,

It's the flames of the sun, the doll answered,

and then she saw a new cavalier,

a black horseman, What is it? Vasilia asked the doll,

It's the blackness,

the doll answered,

of night, the three horsemen

disappeared in the mist, and it started to smell

like damp moss, Baba Yaga had had enough

of Vasilisa and her efficiency and aptitude at household chores,
    Fine, fine,

I'll give you your light, she pulled up one of the skull-lantern spires

and brought it close to Vasilisa,

there was burning coal inside the skull,

steaming through the eye sockets and mouth,

Vasilisa took the spire and walked

home, but when she got

home the house was completely dark, she planted the spire of the
    burning skull

into the earth, she knocked,

the door opened by itself, Where is everybody?

Gone, gone, the doll whispered,
there seemed to have been a curse upon the women
who stayed, when Vasilisa left,
no light, lamps, candles, firewood could pass the threshold of the
    house
without extinguishing, the father was still off,
bartering, grinning, sharing
a tobacco pipe, the step-mother and her daughters died,
trapped
in the darkness of the house, Vasilisa went back outside,
got the skull-lantern and stepped past the threshold,
the cursed threshold, that now let light pass, the bodies
of her step-mother and step-sisters turned to ash
in piles on the floor, the doll told her to bury the flaming skull
in the ground, so it could harm no one else, and advised Vasilisa
to move away from this desolate land
to the big city,

I was eighteen
when I moved out
of our provincial town in America, and ran east, east, east,
take me in my beloved direction,
and above all,
to the city, the liveness of the city (I would have left
earlier if I
legally
could have), the city
was Boston,
then Paris, and now Berlin, but none
were my cities, I've always wanted
a city to love as my own, instead
I dreamt of rats and yellow teeth in dingy apartments (to be fair,
youth is made for
derelict dreams and dingy apartments,
I got my years' worth), Nadyenka says
we can move
back to Paris or anywhere, as long as
we're together, and as long as
we have hot water and electricity
and no war,

we are free,
and we want
to stay free,
Yuri has a friend
whose daughter is a translator from Odessa, she stayed
in Odessa, and in Odessa
the chill came much earlier from the north,
it clipped the days shorter and shorter,
and brought with it darkness,
and that darkness
thickened, they had
no electricity and no hot water, the translator didn't want to leave,
there's a group and they're in it together, translators and writers
in Odessa, they don't want to leave, when the electricity snapped
she put on all the coats she had and continued
translating her text with a flashlight, she'd been working like this
on and off for days, but one morning she went outside
and hailed a cab,
she had no particular destination,
told the cabbie to take a tour of the sites,
as if it were her first time
in Odessa, she leaned her temple
on the cold window
and felt the hot air
from the car heater
float into her lap,


I've been dreaming
of living in a house with a garden somewhere far away
from it all, I've been dreaming
of carrying a child in my belly, I've been trying
to hold my tongue, I've discussed it
so many times with Nadezhda, we just can't
leave each other, so I'll keep that child
in my belly for now, and there's also the issue
of my capacity to withstand
motherhood, with my cognitive behavioural limitations, and I'm
    sometimes afraid

of Nadyenka

as a mother

(the child I would carry, the one she calls 'your child', the one I
    insist

would be 'ours', the one I want to protect

from Nadya's denial of her own pain, I'm also

fucked up, but I'm

in therapy and I take my medication and I'm trying

to face it,

day by day, I'm trying,

for myself and

for the child

who wants to enter my belly, who's waiting for me

and encouraging me

to stay on track, I guess the first thing is, I got to stop

calling myself

fucked up),


Nadya has worked at the same salon (part-time) for nearly a decade,
    just three days a week, but it gives her security, there was
        another hairdresser there,

a handful of years older, from Ukraine, Yulia,

in 2014 it was Nadya's first year at the salon and Yulia

was an old-timer, it was also the year

of Euromaidan, back then

no one cared about Ukraine all that much,

sure, some political analysts and historians

(and Baba Vanga)

chimed in with the warning

that this could become the pivotal global crisis

that it is now, but there wasn't much more than a little buzz, mainly

about the young protesters fighting for a Soviet-free Ukraine at the
    capital,

on Maidan Nezalezhnosti Square or Hrushevsky Street

 (but it didn't go much beyond the photogenic young people and
    tear gas), Yulia left

in the early '90s like most of us, but, from her rent-controlled
    Kreuzberg apartment,

often eulogised her dearest Luhansk, and what

those Ukrainian *dumbasses* (her words) did to such a beautiful city,

she was referring to the war in Donbas between the Russian
   separatists and the Ukrainian nationals that chewed up the city,
   Yulia would release

the locks of the client's hair mid-blow-dry and put her fingers to
   her temples and mumble,

Those savages, everyone is so

twisted in the head, Nadyenka told me, Russians, Ukrainians,
   nobody

knows what's what, especially in the territories

in what we call the Twilight Zone of Donbas,

the Donetsk People's Republic (DPR) and the Luhansk People's
   Republic (LPR),

the sovereign states administered by the Russian civilian-military
   regime, this year

Putin instated them officially into Russia, Yulia

still works at the salon and still

complains about Ukrainian fascists, Yulia

is bonkers, Nadyenka said,

You should hear some of the other stuff she says, Nadya cringed,

I preferred it when Yulia was giving me migraines

with her never-ending stories

about German men

and their big dicks, What about,

Nadya asked her devilishly, the dicks of the men of Luhansk?

Yulia grabbed her chest,

and crinkled her eyes, There's no time, she proclaimed,

for dicks over there,

there's an oblast to protect,


Nadyenka had many business ideas,

mainly hot new beauty products she could

put on the market in Germany, they were all

inspired by Russian products that allowed certain chemical
   ingredients

not legally approved in Europe, Russians are almost as good as the
   Koreans

when it comes to cosmetics and skincare, Nadya told me, of course
   Koreans are the best,

but the European beauty industry just steals and adjusts patents
    from the East, and Nadya
and I really wanted to get rich, the way people who come from
an economic chasm want to get rich, I always hoped I would get
moderately wealthy
from my writing, but then I started to meet
rich people,
really really rich people,
and to be honest I didn't know you could just
do that,
be so rich, I know it's naive,
but I truly believed that kind of wealth
was just an American film and TV narrative, I didn't know
that people,
people in the flesh,
lived like that,
and people do
live like that,
every country has its big-money lifestyle,
I think it never came to me
to want to be rich,
'cause the way that Americans rolled in cash didn't speak to me,
and with French people it's all about old money and titles, but when
    Nadya
told me she wants to be filthy rich, like the nouveau *richniki*,
I thought, if I'm not going to get moderately wealthy nor acclaimed
through my artistic integrity, I might as well reset my dreams to fit
the world as we have it, I'm not sure if it was ever second-degree
for Nadyenka, she just said it without an ounce of shame, but I
    said it
with an ounce of shame,
another Jew who wants money, money, money,
but fuck it,
can't a person want to be rich,
even if that person
is Jewish, even if
there's a war going on? I reviewed
my skill-set, which turned out to be limited
to writing,
specifically, the kind of writing

that provides a limited
earning,
so there was a big gap
between my eyes and the prize,
Nadyenka had skills,
potential money-making skills,
she was lettered-up from medical books and she knew skin and hair
    and kept à jour
with the beauty industry, we decided
it would have to be her
that would get us rich,
'cause other than write a bestseller
(I can't even write 'a seller') all I could do was teach or translate,
    and I wanted
the cosmetic-industry type of cash
plain and simple,
Nadyenka had two products that she was crazy about
that you could only get in Russia,
one was a brow gel (I had never used brow gels before Nadya),
and, let me tell you, this brow gel sleeks
the eyebrows like I've never known my eyebrows to be,
aligns and shapes and holds the form all day,
I underestimated how much a sleek eyebrow can exalt the face,
there are many brow gels on the market, Nadya told me
she's tried them all, and nothing, I tell you, nothing
holds a candle
to this brow gel, the other product that got her fired up
was this enzyme body peel in powder form, Nadyenka explained
how special and singular it was, it went
over my head, but there was this determinate chemical
that was not legal in Europe, that did something like
burn the top layer of your skin – can't get youth
without a good burn, according to Nadyenka –
she had an idea about how to replicate the contents
and replace that ingredient with two others that would
produce the same effect, she even ran it
by a chemist friend, though very vaguely,
'cause she was sure that he'd steal it if he got wise to the details, in
    retrospect,
I think she explained to me a bit vaguely as well for the same reason,

she actually never even wrote down the ingredient list in full, just
    kept it
in her head, that way no one
could heist it from her (a leitmotif in her life,
I give people everything, she often said,
and then they run off with it), Listen, baby, she told me,
we need a cash cow idea and didn't I tell you
I was your cow, she winked, God,
she's got that wink down, You are,
I flushed, my sexy cow,
we grabbed at each other
ironically,
but I was a little
turned on,
by the joke of our flesh
and the thrill of a sustainable future,
So now, Nadya continued, we just need
the start-up cash, I've got no money to put in, I told Nadyenka,
I've got a little, she said, but I've been putting it aside
each month
for us,
and it's not enough yet,
but I'll just keep going,
and I think we can get something off its feet with a couple thousand,
okay, five thousand, I don't have five thousand, I said,
I don't even have half, unless I break my savings, and those savings
are all I have 'cause I don't have
anything for retirement, I was already ready
to throw in the towel,
I really hate thinking business, which is a problem
for getting rich, but Nadyenka had that economist hope and patience,
she was determined to have the life
she wanted and give me the life
I began to want with her, Nadyenka dreamed
of having her own spa, and then developing a line of products
that were a limited edition and could only be purchased through
    her spa,
something along the lines of Susanne Kaufmann, the Austrian who
    inherited a spa in the Alpine region of the Bregenzerwald, she
    had a line of luxury skincare

only available at the spa,
then it got so popular clients travelled through the rolling hills just
    to get another jar of the Restorative Toning Cream or vile of
    the Nutrient Serum, she put
the whole shelf on the market and BAM! but she was
already rich, Nadyenka told me not to focus
on our minuses, I felt like we had mostly
minuses, but Nadyenka swore
her enzyme peel will be better than Kaufmann's, and I started
believing it, and believing
is the real investment capital, metaphysics
has always been the means
for people like us,

I was often tempting Nadya
to throw pity parties
about our poor upbringing, her father first
worked at a supermarket, he stole
candy bars for Nadyenka from there, the manager
knew and turned a blind eye, sometimes Nadyenka would come to
    the store
and help her father restock, everyone liked Nadya, she was
    beautiful and behaved,
had long silken hair that she made sure to always have well-brushed,
spoke German with impeccable politeness, my father's
first job was at McDonald's, I was not
that pretty, all right that's maybe a loose piece of glitter
from my own pity party, children are beautiful,
all children are so beautiful, youth is immense and overriding,
I did not believe in my youth, I was not taught
to believe in my youth, my papa
brought home extras from his shift,
burgers and fries and chicken nuggets and we cut them up and
    munched on them
alongside the bowl of borscht, the teachers told my parents
I was getting picked on
because of my clothes and they should consider
getting me some American clothes, they did not have the money
for American clothes, even thrift store prices
were not a given back then, I fixated on the brand names

embroidered on the other children's tees and hoodies,
they were so cool, I spoke
English with impeccable politeness, Nadyenka and I were
were both keeping our chins up
as we translated the world to our parents, a world my mama
explained to me in detail after I had
translated it to her in detail, we couldn't talk back,
we weren't like the overindulged Americans or the contemptuous
    Germans,
there was strict generational etiquette, we were talking on the
    phone,
I was in England giving a lecture and she was home in Berlin doing
    makeup,
she told me that there is still
so much room in the world
for us,

we have been together
for so long, I have known you
for so long, and you have known me
for so long, and those years are folded into the months
we have spent
together, it is dark
here on Ilsestraße, fifth floor,
in the darkest hour of the darkest day of a Berlin black-milk winter,
    Nadyenka
hasn't changed her clothes, she just took off
her wool hat and cashmere scarf and big bomber jacket, they are
    all damp
because it snowed and melted, she hung them
in the bathroom
on the heaters, she came
into the bedroom where
I was sitting, I had heard her come in,
but I didn't greet her, didn't get up or even say anything at all, she
    knew
where I was anyways, and why I was
quiet, she was also quiet, the loudest things
were the squeak of the boots on the wooden floor as she set them
    down

and they slid, and the weight of the coat as it slid
off her sleeve by sleeve and bounced mid-air,
the way the zipper banged against
the radiator when it was
hung up and the final flick
of the light switch when Nadya agreed to the darkness
and came into the bedroom
and sat
beside me,

my father's half Moldav, half Romanian,
Nadyenka says she has a great-grand-babushka who's Ukrainian,
 but
she was a bitch,
apparently, otherwise
Nadyenka is part of that snow-white lineage, her mother's uncle's
 dedushka
was a fisherman from the Tersky coast, on the shores of the White
 Sea
with its pale-yellow arctic light, Kashkarantsy was the town, he was
a burly lone-wolf, he thrived
on the rugged conditions of the far north,
icicles in his metallic beard, shack of strung-up fish, he dried
and packed and sold to the southern oblasts, there's a short
poem by the Romanian poet Mariana Marin called 'Destiny',
she died in 2003 when I was at the legal age to vote
and join the army, instead I moved out
of my parents' place and went east
to the American coast, Mariana speaks of two people
who were in love, and why
they were in love, they were
in love 'cause they shared the exact same
fear and experienced the exact same
cruelty,
my Romanian dedushka's family
is from Galați, it used to be part of Moldova, but then became
Romanian 1918, my Moldav babushka who didn't know how to
 read or write
escaped to the other side of the Danube (the Moldav side)
for a job as a maid, she falsified

her documents to say she was seventeen,
she was a mature fifteen, but already had the rough hands, she
    came with us
to America, my papa said he wouldn't leave
without her, mama's boy, she was
far from grateful, not because she did not appreciate the way my
    papa
would break his back for her, but because life
is hard, and to behave otherwise
would betray the toil of sixty years,
better to break a back
than to admit a broken belief system,
when we buried her
we didn't know her real age anymore,
the family went with the number
on her American passport, she, herself, had forgotten over the years,
it may have given her
one or two extra
years of life, she was petite
with chestnut hair and open-field-blue eyes,
very Moldav,
her husband had yellow eyes and bronze hair, my papa
had yellow eyes and bronze hair, I have
yellow eyes and bronze hair, okay dark bronze,
okay, brown, dark brown,
once in Paris I studied with a Romanian guy named Mihai,
he was straight, but, in a future
more deconstructed generation, he would be
genderless, I really liked him and he really liked me,
in that human way, he knew
I was a dyke, Romanians,
like Ukrainians can be quite culturally patriotic,
when I told him I was a quarter Romanian, he said,
You're full Romanian! he took me in his arms and I took him
in my arms, I've never been full
anything national, and I felt
at home with him, he invited me
to his home, he was from Bucharest, It's a beautiful city, he told
    me, and it
will see your beauty, that's how he spoke, Come home, my sister,

I needed a brother so bad,
he said he'd take me to my ancestral town of Galați, I had started
planning the trip with him,
I needed a home so bad,
Mihai had an older sister,
she had a husband and a four-year-old, Mihai showed me photos
of the little rascal, his big chocolate eyes
and light brown curls that bounced onto his forehead, he never
showed me photos
of the husband, said he hated
that son-of-a-bitch, but couldn't convince his sister to leave
the bum, the husband had never raised his hand
to his sister, Mihai almost wished that he had,
so he would have had proof, he spoke so delicately, even when he
    swore, he told me
that bastard screwed up her head,
and he couldn't get his sister to admit that
her husband terrorised her, but Mihai saw how she became
nervous, clumsy, faltered,
in Romania
it's not so easy to go to the police
(it's not easy anywhere, I told him),
sometimes he reminded of me of Arturchik,
Mihai was part of a human rights group in Bucharest, he was
    especially impassioned
by the advocacy for women's rights, in 2010, he told me,
over half of Romanians agreed that women provoked
their own beatings, in his
beloved Romania, in our
beloved Romania,
Mihai and I wanted to go
after the semester ended, May or June,
in early April, the birds were already full-on,
we had a couple of classes to go, and then
we'd take our trip, Mihai and I, we were just waiting on some final
details to get the tickets,
he didn't show up
to class,
I went over to Mihai's apartment
above the Montmartre cemetery

off the stinky metro line thirteen, he said that he couldn't
feel his hands, I asked him
if he wanted me to
hold him, he said, Yes, even though he didn't lift
a limb when I did,
his sister
didn't leave a note,
she was in the bathtub, her son knocked
as he was told and waited for his mama
to say come in, as he was told,
his father was strict
about that kind of stuff,
the boy kept rasping his little knuckles on the door,
there was no answer and he really needed
to pee, he turned the handle and he did
pee,
Mihai said the piece-of-shit
will get custody of the boy, his parents
can't do anything because it's the law,
and Mihai can't even explain it to his parents,
who keep saying that she had always been
like this, very sick, very sad,
Mihai had the faith of ten fighters
in justice, I borrowed his faith
often, he went to Bucharest alone,
we messaged and talked briefly on the phone a couple times
(we are both not
phone people, though we both
made an effort), it took months,
he kept postponing his flight back, he became spotty, he was my
    brother,
I was his sister, he had a sister,
and then he didn't, and I had him,
and then I didn't,


my mama's friend back in Kharkiv, Shurka, who helped me with
    my Ukrainian birth certificate
did these road trips in 2014,
well, it was more like humanitarian aid, but Shurka was a cowboy
    at heart,

she'd say, It's time to hit the road, her four-door Skoda type, the
    bumper sagged
and one of the windshield wipers didn't work, but otherwise she'd
    been keeping that car
in real good shape, she hit it on the trunk twice
for good luck before she revved it up, Let's go, Old Boy,
it was late February, freezing
even in the south that
suddenly no longer belonged
to Ukraine, she collected tents and batteries and clean underwear
and food, there was a Ukrainian boy at the border
who traded his tank for a glass of milk,
it had been weeks, there was nothing
to put in your mouth but
rubble, Shurka went
from Kharkiv to the towns around, and had a call-trail
of donations she picked up along the way, she was very social,
Shurka, and made everyone she talked to
feel like a hero, it was sincere,
she believed in heroism, not
that it's rare and almighty, but that it could never
belong to anyone, though of course she still greeted friends
and cashiers and mechanics (who were all her friends too) with
*Geroyem Slava, Ukraini Slava* (Glory to the Heroes, Glory to Ukraine),
as every decent Ukrainian was expected to,
and she was hardcore for her country, she saw
a kid die on a stretcher
holding a purple teddy bear, the bear was missing
an arm, the girl was missing
her stomach, the parents were
so young Shurka thought
they were her brother and sister, there was frost everywhere
as she held the wheel in her thick lamb's wool gloves
(the heater in Old Boy was acting up),
down to Armiansk where her friend Grisha loaded up her supplies
in his truck to take the rest of the way,
she spent the night, and Grisha got someone to take a look at her heater,
and, by morning, he had it fixed, and she thanked him,
and he thanked her, and he was on his way,
and she took Old Boy back north,

it was too late
for the region, clean underwear
was no match for Russia's military, the Ukrainian soldiers
retreated to the military base, they guarded it behind the fence,
they were ordered not
to shoot, to stand
firm and non-reactive,
the Russian officers went right up
to the wire hive and, man by man,
they spit through the chinks
onto the chins and noses and foreheads and eyes
of the Ukrainian *soldati* who had already
surrendered,
there are perhaps two main
unexplainable phenomenon in life,
war
and love
(though Mama has explained both
to me in painstaking detail), Nadyenka's mama,
who claims she is not a political person,
then makes it a point to bring up the war
at the dinner table, has a dulcet, dove-like voice, I can't imagine
her hitting Nadyenka as a child, I try to remind myself
who she has been to Nadya while she slides more beef *pelmyeni*
onto my plate, and tops up the sour cream on the side, she is
a violent woman, I tell myself, she tells me
softly that I should please help myself, she has more
on the stove, she serves Nadya with the same
gentleness, though Nadya reminds me often that her mama hates
the fact that she has put on weight, Nadyenka was always
her little ballerina, Who wants to be a ballerina, I tell Nadya,
when they can be a dyke? I wink
at the end of my phrase, I'm not
good at winking but I'm trying it out, I don't want to die
without improving
my wink, Nadya's mama is talking about a war
that doesn't exist, she refers to it as it should be referred to,
as she claimed, not as a war, but a special operation,
she likes my earrings,
and hates fake media, she was on vacation in Spain

last spring with her husband, they rented a car and went up the
     coast starting at Malaga,
they got lost in one of the mountain towns looking for a church,
they ran into Ukrainians at the square,
and had a chat, and her mama refilled my glass with sparkling water,
she's always wearing these linen dresses
that are a bit see-through,
the gap between her skinny legs in full view,
she told me the Ukrainians they met in Spain
told both her and her husband
that the truth is, Ukrainians want to be free
of fascism,
they want a better economy,
bigger retirement fund,
quality healthcare, and so on, and Russia
can give them this,
her mama said that they were so nice,
and she was glad they all
understood that Russia
was only trying to help, and these Ukrainians
helped her mama and papa find the church,
her mama added that the woman had
such pretty shoes, and that she wished
that she could still wear heels,
Nadyenka's face was getting red, her mama said,
Nadya, your face is getting red,
I like Ukrainians, her mama said,
and touched my shoulder
with a feather-light hand,



a fuzzy grey kitten
is sliding across a linoleum floor
on the screen of a mobile phone
in a mittened hand
on the floor of a metro station
full of sleeping bags,
the whole world could fit into his wide eyes, Tymor
is Yuri's friend, a gentle faggot in bumblefuck Novosibirsk

who can't leave his severely autistic uncle
and super-old grandma (his mama
died last year and his father's been out of the picture for a while,
there's no other family), the Russian-speaking queer organisation
    here, where
Nadya volunteers,
was trying to get him out, he can't live
with himself
if he leaves,
and Lilyechka – she's not anyone's cousin
but someone in the organisation was trying to prove
that she was, our *sladenkaya* Lilyechka –
*Ukrainochka ridna* from Kyiv's Podol district trying to cross the border
    into Poland
with papers that say she's male, she loves her country
but she needs her oestrogen,

I had my elbows
on the table, Nadyenka's mama
asked me again
if I wanted more,

in north-east Ukraine, the snake bites its own tail
on the borderlands, Russian bombs
blast Moscow Avenue
located in Ukrainian Kharkiv, it's since
been renamed
Heroes of Kharkiv Avenue, there's a nineteen-year-old girl
on the thirty-four trolly bus going north towards Saltivka,
coming home with a chin wet from the smudged tears
of another date gone wrong, she's more worried she'll never
find *the one* than about
death by bomb shelling, the girl she met was so different
than her online photos, it's not that she's vain,
but discrepancies make her freeze, she's scared
to be touched, she has been
as long as she can remember, her friends are all
touchy-feely, boyfriends and girlfriends, she wants
to be like them or
like anyone other than

herself, it's hard
for her to deal with disappointment, she has to make sure
she doesn't look like she's been
crying, then she can just go straight to her room,
and use the safety pin she keeps in her jewellery box
to prick her thighs, she can't tell
her parents yet, her brother is on active duty,
her father is a physical therapist, the clinic was always understaffed,
but now it's daily Sisyphean call sheets, kids, adults,
civilians, service men and women, babushkas and dedushkas,
prosthetics and rehabilitation take time and patience, he only
    sees
his daughter when she's sleeping,
or he thinks she's sleeping, it's just that
it's nighttime and her door is closed,
she's relieved to be back
in the city, after staying with her grandparents
during the evacuation, she'd much rather
lay with this despair
in her own bed,

it is our bed, the bed we share,
Nadezhda and I, even if it's in the same bedroom
where she slept
with her ex-wife, she bought
new sheets, I like washed linen,
she prefers cotton, linen is scratchy, rough
on the skin, I like that,
Nadya doesn't, she kept
the same mattress, I wanted a new one,
not sentimentally, but one that was just bigger,
my bed in Paris is big, maybe too big
for my small apartment, it's the most expensive
thing I own, and it's served me well
during my severe depressive episodes, it's great for
sleeping and not being able to sleep,
and for crying, my pillows are expensive too,
if I'm going to have perpetual red eyes,
I might as well have a well-rested spine,
her bed is an odd size, I don't know if it's a German size,

it's bigger than a twin, and if it's a double
the name is deceiving, it's meant for one person in my opinion,
Nadezhda gets very defensive when I bring it up,
she was always trying to fit two people into one,
the only way to sleep in her bed is to
hold each other, the nights when
holding each other
is the last thing I or she wanted to do
(it is usually just me, she
seems to never lose her taste for holding, I also
love to be held, clutched, squeezed,
the tighter the grip, the more I exist), I didn't receive much
physical touch as a child, actually
close to none, my parents say otherwise,
but they were both given
less than I was,
I was a child who
avoided touch, the other kids took it
as a challenge, they ran after me,
whoever could catch me
in their bear hug won, I learned
to run fast, but they had strategy,
and multiple feet outrun just two, the American teacher said
it's just a hug, hugs are nice,
it went dark inside me,
the darkest hour of the darkest day,
how many times have I been
buried alive?
I'm afraid of small spaces, the small space that's created
between two sets of skin, I can't stand
being dead without dying,
my mother said it's fine
to not want to be touched, she also didn't like
to be touched, not everyone wants to be touched,
but I did
want to be touched,

I feel free,
and I don't take my freedom
for granted, though it became a problem

when I stopped wanting sex and started wanting
a hug,
I didn't know how to go about it
and I couldn't ask anyone, rather
I didn't have anyone to ask,
everyone I knew
knew me
as a tough, cold, hermitted,
I flaunted it from a young age,
I was not afraid of death,
could give a fuck, go ahead,
kill me, it was almost a party trick,
in my mid-twenties my brain
took a swerve, and I became
skittish, scattered, a different person,
I didn't get it, but, then again,
I didn't get much of anything back in the day,
I refused to see a therapist
(not that anyone was proposing,
I just liked proclaiming
that I wouldn't go)
and then the angels or God
or whatever it was that gave faith to people
in places like concentration camps, sent me
a friend,

that friend held me
forever, and I
rose from my grave,

I read Yevgeny Yevtushenko's poem 'Babi Yar'
too much, I was trying to stop
hurting myself physically
(this time around with much more progress
thanks to the cognitive behavioural therapy),
I had to replace my craving with something,
and the closest thing to a knife
is a poem,
I read poems
that cut into me,

about the devastated
human spirit,
I needed my fix, Yevtushenko was not a Jew,
but wrote one of the bravest and most devoted poems
in honour of Jews (it was not
à la mode to support Jews,
to say the least), it was a poem about a ravine in Kyiv
that is now a flat field
'cause it was filled
with executed Jewish corpses,
the two days in September were mild, row by row
line-ups at the edge
of the ravine where crowds
of deported Ukrainian Jews awaited
their relocation, the *Einsatzkommando*
reported the success of the firing squads
to the higher-ups,
nearly 34,000 Jews
share one bed,

I like Jews, Nadyenka tells me,
her German education, memorial visits, the class projects
dedicated to Anne Frank, the Shoah survivor lectures,
the Soviet silence stretches like the steppes,
they gave their Jews away, twenty years
after the Babi Yar massacre, 1961, still
no commemoration, no monument, just part of the lot
of soil that holds no names, Yevtushenko wrote
'Babi Yar', he was not
a Jew, but proclaimed that in the eyes of every
anti-Semite he is Jewish,
(long before *Je suis Charlie*),
the opening lines state
that there is no monument on that ravine,
he called out to his country, his
beloved country,
to take responsibility,
to honour the dead, our dead,
our Jewish dead, our people,
our beloved people with whom

we share a motherland,
it became one of the most well-known poems
of the century (a year later
Shostakovich even set this poem to music
in his thirteenth Symphony, and it was first performed
on a milk-dark winter in Moscow, but for fifty years
no official commemoration, in 1991,
the year my family left Soviet Ukraine,
just before it became
an independent country, the names
were recorded, Yevtushenko died
in Tulsa, Oklahoma, not
in his beloved motherland,
I like Jews, Nadezhda tells me,
in the first weeks we go on dates,
we talk about our parents, we share
the Soviet Union, we talk
in short-cuts, she understands,
I don't have to explain why
no one could leave, the food lines,
the bribes, the thin-lipped gossip that could land you
in prison, my mom is exceptionally
smart, I tell her, she studied applied mathematics,
was at the top of her class, Then why,
Nadyenka asks with the gentlest
voice, did your mama end up going to night school rather than
one of the top universities? my mouth
doesn't close, the last century
slides down my shoulders, Because,
I say, a bit dumbfounded, she's Jewish,
And? Nadyenka asks, I don't understand
Nadyenka's translucent eyes, so peaceful
and open, I tell her Jews were barred
from those kind of schools
(except in the cases of ties and money),
Were they? Nadyenka asks, I don't understand
how we shared this country of ours,
this Soviet country of ours, and
it's news to her, that my papa
got the shit beat out of him weekly in his neighbourhood

for being Jewish, though the neighbours said
it was just horseplay, then my papa,
age ten, bulked up until he had pecks
and was not afraid to pick up a piece of wood,
and whack someone in the face with it
if need be, it's news to her
that Jews were kept out of
schools, jobs, housing,
it's news to her, that my babushka
wouldn't let me part my hair in the middle, though I begged,
'cause Svetochka and Masha had their hair like that, all the girls
     had their
hair like that, but Babushka said it drew too much attention
to my big nose, I like your nose,
Nadyenka smiles merrily and touches my cheek,
I close my mouth,
all I can say is,
I like my nose too,

They'll say I ran, Pasha whispered,
I didn't run,

there's a joke
about joking,
and it goes like this:
a judge exits his chambers trying to catch his breath
he's laughing so hard tears stream from his eyes,
his puffed cheeks are rosy and he puts his hand on the bald spot
     of his head
and slides it down his face, whimpering into his palm with joy,
a judicial colleague spots him from the hallway and approaches,
he asks the judge what's making him bellow with such laughter,
I just heard, the judge answers between chuckles,
the funniest joke in the whole entire world,
Oh please, the colleague steps closer,
tell me, I love jokes,
the judge's face stills, his cheeks sag on his serious expression, I
     can't,
the judge replies,
I just sent someone to Siberia for it,

there's a tactic to expansion, you clear
the land and repopulate it
with your own, like Russia did with the coast by the White Sea,
with the Finns and Estonians, or the deportation
of the Balkars, Chechens, Ingush, Crimean Tatars, Karachays,
    Meskhetian Turks,
the forced settlement programs, the Sovietisation
of Siberia, indigenous communities, the Koryaks, Nenets,
Chukchi, Yukaghir, Evenks, Kets, Khanty, Mansi, Sakha,
the name Siberia comes from the Tatar word meaning
'Sleeping land',
vast, wild, and dark, these cultures
knew the land, its animal- and plant-life,
it only became barbaric when barbars arrived,
there was a language to the natural territory,
there were shamans, and the earth had a voice,
the deer had a voice, the bear had a voice,
there was a process to creating new settlements, in the 1930s,
compulsory boarding schools for indigenous children
removed from their families, forbidden to speak
their native language or practice
their native traditions, there was
the abduction and execution of community leaders,
there were strict laws to civilise the rest,
owning a drum would get you
executed,

meanwhile, in the 1930s
in the Sovietised western territories,
Yasha's father conceived a great way
to kill off a nation
under the name of
agriculture,
part of Ukraine's wealth was its soil,
its beloved soil, new laws
for the so-called sake of fairly sharing resources
obliged the confiscation of Ukrainian grain production,
the golden fields, wheat and corn, that grow
so well, stocked and transferred into Russia, soldiers
went into homes

and boxed-up household groceries,
methodologically skimming
all food sources from the people, a man-made
famine, the *Holodomor*,
meaning kill by starvation,
it was no secret,
the world watched and the world saw,
international aid was continuously offered,
and continuously rejected
by the Soviet government,
who watched and who saw,
the NKVD now KGB
still have control of the archives,
but scholars estimate
between three and a half to eight million
Ukrainians starved to death
in peacetime,
with an abundance of food,

Nadyenka and I like to dance
to kitsch Russian techno pop from the '90s,
maybe it's that Gorbachev gap where you could go far
with innuendo, it's always cheesy and tragic
and about love,
it was a time when Nadya and I bumped heads a lot
over every little thing, and being hurt
the way we each had been hurt, we hadn't yet found
a way to make our childhood pain compatible,
it was an awful time,
the days were particularly long,
the damned sun would never set
and we got dark
at each other
over a dirty floor,
a missed call, a wrong look,

I wanted to leave her,
I hated her
apartment, her city, her ringtone,
but then a halo of time would be bestowed upon us,

five minutes, a half an hour, never more
than half a day, where I couldn't think of anyone else
I'd rather be miserable with,
we were blind
together,
and I didn't want to see
the world anymore
on my own,
overall, it was a time when,
to give our nervous systems a break,
we opted for the subject
of love
rather than the experience,
nothing got us in the mood to be safely emotional
as the vicarious dance-heartbreak beats of Gosti iz Budushchego
(Guests from the Future),
Yura Usachov and Eva Polna, the duo
from Saint Pete, homo icons, of course
I had a crush on Eva Polna, of course
I didn't tell Nadya,
though who didn't have a crush on Eva Polna,
singular or universal,
the topic of crushes always led us
to misreckoning and hyperventilation
for one or both parties, we sung
our guts out to 'Ne Lyubov' (Not
Love), about a lover who obviously lacks
boundaries, makes the singer their world, their life,
their fever, this kind of love
is killing the singer
in various ways, mainly
that the lover is in love
with their own love,

Nadya and I were jumping around the living room,
kicking up dust, and then the chorus came
and we turned to each other and belted,
*Not Love! Not Love! Not Love!*,

there was our favourite, 'Begi ot menya' (Run
from me), which was the song with the lesbians

in the video, super-hot era
of metallic lipstick and reaching out towards the camera
amidst a trashy strobe array,
where everything that needed to be said
was said against a wall,
or with a sharp head turn,
and let me tell you, the two female lovers in the video
turned their head a lot
towards each other
then looked away, it was
ultimate lesbian nomenclature,
somehow chic with solitude and femininity, 'Run
from me' was full
of mixed signals, kiss
don't kiss, call don't call, I love
songs that so clearly exhibit
a complete lack
of secure and constructive communication,
it was a guilty pleasure to utter
unexamined things to music as if
I had never been
to therapy, the chorus
is *Cry, cry,*
*dance, dance,*
and I don't know any culture
that mixes party time with despair
as well as the Slavs (except, naturally,
the Jews), dancing
was a great alternative to sex
for Nadya and I, in the beginning
she always asked me to sit on her face,
I'd face the wall and press my palms against it
and she'd shove her tongue
inside me and
suck on my clit (she loved
sucking, personally
it wasn't my favourite,
too much pressure, but I let her suck it a bit,
and then told her
to mostly lick above it – that was the best), when I ask her

if she's horny, she tells me
she's been waiting for me
to drip into her mouth
all day, though
sometimes she answers, No,
and if we both feel secure with that,
we let it be, and if I hesitate with my expression,
she quickly adds, But I'll
fuck you good tomorrow, I prefer
just the No, I don't want to be fucked good
tomorrow, I want to be honest
today,

there was a massacre that was bigger
than Babi Yar in Odessa and the towns of Transnistria,
which at that time was controlled by Romania,
my beloved Romania, to speed things up
the chosen people were chosen
and brought to a barracks,
the floor was pre-covered
with gasoline, the firing squad
shot, and then they burned the mass
around 5 p.m., Romanian soldiers and the SS
wiped out an estimated 30,000 people,
mostly Ukrainian Jews,
in what is now known as the Odessa Massacre,

Nadya and I were dancing in Berlin
to Eva Polna's crooning
instead of fucking good, we were
being honest with each other,
she had made her own pesto
that night, our off-key yowls
smelled of garlic, we kissed many times,
sometimes with tongue, though
none were sexual kisses,
we put our oily lips together and shared broken cords,
it was our way
of making promises,

I had not brought many
books with me to Berlin, I chose essentials,
the ones that I needed like
the medication I need today,
the one that's on the floor in the bedroom, on my side,
next to my balled-up socks, it's slim
with a peach-rose cover, bent and water-worn
from reading in the bath
and hanging on to it in the rain, it rained
a lot in Paris, blotchy drops that just wobbled out of the clouds,
and took even the meteorologists by surprise, the pages
were Ilya Kaminsky's poetry collection, *Dancing in Odessa*,
I had held on to it through eight countries, two of which
I lived in, I managed to get it back
from an ex who lived in London,
and had a very different
understanding about the terms of our break-up, in the title poem,
'Dancing in Odessa', a deaf boy
counts the birds in his neighbour's backyard
and dials that number, professing his love
to the stranger on the other end, Kaminsky lost
his hearing when he was four,
his family got political asylum and moved to
America in 1993, he began writing poems
in English
so that his family
wouldn't be able to understand them, language is
a bedroom everyone has, with a door
you can close
and lock, the music
in his stanzas
comes from an instrument
not yet invented, I kept this thin
book
as I kept myself,
I, too,
want to write in a language
that doesn't yet exist,
Baba Vanga has sand

in her eyes, Ilya Kaminsky has sand
in his ears, I've got sand
in my mouth,
the earth is not
round, it's an hourglass,

Nadyenka and I also went
to Spain together,
to a small town south of Málaga,
not the one where her parents
met the Ukrainians who allegedly patted Putin on the back,
and helped Nadya's mama and papa
find the church, but a different town,
it was accessible by train, I drive,
Nadyenka doesn't, but we didn't rent
a car, I was not feeling confident
in my body, let alone
in a vehicle, I had this outlandish fear
that I'd run someone over,
though I had no need
for speed, I was
an easy-does-it driver, but it felt
like a premonition, Maybe
you also see the future, Nadyenka said,
I do believe in paranormal gifts, but personally
I think my fears are the least
informed source of truth,
I'd rather rely on tarot, coffee grinds,
or an astrology vlogger than
the suppositions that my mind makes up
(and I have put my trust
in all three, with some form
of success, a tarot reading saved me
from a trip to Norway
for a girl who had
many last straws
to lay upon my back,
coffee grinds
told me to come home
when my mama had her hysterectomy,

an astrology vlogger with whom
I paid for a private session
read me my angel cards,
it was the first time I had the thought
that there was perhaps
another way out,
– it would be years before I followed through
with Jungian vigour), my projected guilt
of vehicular homicide was most likely
a Krzysztof Kieślowskian doubling,
myself behind the wheel
and myself stepping out into traffic,

we slept in late
every morning, from our rented apartment
we could hear the waves
of the Alboran Sea
round and flatten, brushing
the shore, we were not in a hurry,
it was a wonderful quality
that we both shared, though we both
leaned towards depressive episodes,
but here we were not
depressed, we were something like
happy
to be away,
for once, not because we were running
away,
even though they say,
if you leave a place young
you'll run again,

there was a pet store that sold puppies and kittens
in the town, we stumbled upon it
while walking in circles,
taking our time picking out keychains
only to change our minds last minute,
and walk on, there it was,
the store window framed with chips of azure tiling,
the shutter lowered to cover most of the front window,

just enough to see a couple of cottony tails and squished sleepers,
nose beneath their tummy, we had assumed it was closed,
but the owner explained the sun was too hot, that's why he lowered
all the blinds,
there were two rooms, he asked *gatos* or *perros*
we said *gatos*, he spoke no English,
and I mean no English,
not even Hello or Goodbye, just long strings of Spanish,
we responded back with chunks of English and French that we
    curved
and added o's to, his name was Domingo,
like the day, I assumed, I knew *Domingo* meant Sunday,
but Domingo put his hands together in prayer
and pointed to the ceiling, turns out
*Domingo* also means the Lord,
and his shop, called Patitas,
did not mean fried potatoes, as we had originally deduced (how cute,
by why fried?), but Little Paws,
Nadya and I
were categorically against pet shops,
but when Domingo came out with two copper-haired kittens
in each hand and extended them to us
we took the wiggly things,
and piety descended upon our souls, inside
there were stacked cages, all puppies,
he told us to follow him, the second room, more
stacked cages, all kittens,
it was horrible, vicious, cruel, we wanted
all the kittens, every single one,
Domingo closed the door, Watch this, we think he said,
and opened up all the cage doors, the kittens poured out,
squeezing meows, nibbles, slipping and falling, wet noses, baby
    whiskers,
I could have married Nadyenka
and forgiven the Soviet Union, we crouched down,
the kittens battled towards us, jumping up and sliding off our
    knees,
I picked up three at once, I don't know what face I was making,
but it was one I had not, in my near-forty years of life, ever made
    before,

soon we gathered that he was not performing a magic trick,
but needed to clean the cages and could use a couple hands
to play with the kittens while he changed the newspaper and refilled
    their
water bowls, we were kissing as many furry foreheads as we could,
some of them smelled like pee or poop,
but also like vanilla bean and warm milk, Domingo
told us that we could have one for 250 or, if we wanted two,
he could make a deal, each kitten comes
with all its vaccines
and a passport, safe for travel, Nadya
doesn't even have an EU passport, I hesitated
to make a joke of it,
our baby kitten
would have European nationality
before her, but the kernel
in my belly shivered,
my other baby, the one waiting for me
to get good
with myself,
there is a seed inside me
begging, Please
let me come out
of the darkness,
we turned down
Domingo's emphatic offers and his mouth sank, he hunched
down to the floor and began
putting all the kittens back
in their cages by the handfuls, we left,
our flip-flops smacking
on the hot red-bricked sidewalk, we walked
back to the apartment, the kitchen
was cool, we finished the slices of melon
and jamón we had in the fridge,
We can't,
Nadyenka said with her mouth full,
a layer of orange
spread across the sky,
I knew she wasn't
just talking about the kittens,

Pasha
has a tattoo of a kitten
on his throat, on the left side, just an outline
with whiskers, and a curled-in tail, it's really cute,
with his shaved head and silver earring
on the left lobe it makes him look
oddly rowdy, it's his jaw or his sunken eyes,
or that sharp Adam's apple, he's wearing
a button-down with a tie and some old Reebok zip-up over it,
it's very Berlin, chapped lips and a slit eyebrow,
– he cut the slit on the right brow several times
until it scarred, and no hair grew on the wormy line –
Pasha
hasn't taken opiates
since he was a teen
back in Chicago
where his family immigrated
the same year as mine, all three of us,
Nadya, Pasha, and I,
seven-year-olds in the sky
westbound, but he stopped,
he cut it all out, and now he never
takes anything, not even aspirin, ibuprofen, acetaminophen,
he once broke his leg
doing something stupid
with all his soul, he was already in Berlin,
he called me from the hospital,
and I called Nadya, we both came
Nadya translated, both Pasha and I
spoke the little German that we spoke
like the act of speaking itself was something we had never learned,
Nadyenka told the doctor he can't have any painkillers,
he's a recovered addict, the doctor said, I understand,
and they put a mouth guard in and fixed up his leg
without an ounce of anything, Pasha near-shattered
his teeth clenching down on that guard,
but got through it, even I pleaded, Pasha,
maybe just take something, we'll be here,
we won't let you
go bad,

neither Nadya nor I
had been addicts, Pasha's leg
healed just fine, and he said he'd stop
proclaiming his love to boys
from the tops of cars, the boy in question
dropped him off at the hospital (it was his car on which
Pasha proclaimed), but left as soon as Pasha
was signed in, Guess it wasn't
mutual, Pasha mumbled, his hospital gown
was pulled up on one side and I could see a sliver
of his hairy pale thigh,
he had to keep the knee slightly bent
because of the cast, is there anything
more vulnerable on a man than
his bare hairy thigh,
his mama
had gotten in contact with him, told him
his papa was asking questions, Let him
ask questions, Pasha said,

he came
to stay with me in Paris, he told me
I could always find him
in the darkness that filled me, when darkness
filled me, he would sit there
with me, I'm not afraid
of all that, if you want to kill yourself you
call me and tell me
how you plan on doing it, and I'll
give you tips, we both joked a lot
about suicide, like how
you can't rely on anyone these days,
even to die, you have to do it yourself,

I had never
completed an attempt, he had
two under his belt, both with pills,
they were back in those days, when he didn't know
the sky from the ground,
he held my hands

in his hands, and recited Mayakovsky, the lines
about the stars being specs of spit, and the poem
addressed to the future, 'To All and Everything',
I loved
Mayakovsky, but could never memorise
his verse, they say
those who remember the beginnings
are idealists,
and those who remember the endings
aren't the type to complete
an attempt, I just remember the ending
of the poem, not for the words
but for the voice
that swam out of Pasha
for dear life, *To you*
*my great souls, I bequeath*
*the orchard.*

Pasha
had a brother
who died, it was back in Ukraine,
his brother was older and Pasha
was younger, five, six,
and Lyosha was fourteen, he was from
his father's first wife,

Pasha is crazy about
salami sandwiches, Nadya can eat salami slices
like chips, I also love salami, but got in the habit
of saying, No, thanks, 'cause I was worried
about my cholesterol (weak hearts run in my family),
there was this *multik* from the '70s,
a cartoon called *Uncle Fedya, His Dog, and His Cat*,
neither Nadya nor I knew it, Pasha knew it
from Lyosha, there's Fedya,
a young boy who's precocious, he gets called 'uncle'
because of his maturity and intelligence, he can read
at age four, and cook for himself
at age six (how often the outcome of neglect is called
'maturity and intelligence'), Fedya feels most understood

by animals, one day
he comes across a talking stray
cat, he brings the kitty home,
but his mother says, No way no how,
and kicks the cat out, so Fedya decides
to run away
with his new cat friend
who he names Matroskin (Seaman), they take the bus
away from the city
and get off at a village
named Prostokvashino (Soured Milk), where they find,
by chance, an empty house, This
is our new home, Fedya is happy
with Matroskin, he's young
but self-sufficient, so no problemo, in the village
of Soured Milk he befriends
a talking dog, who likes Fedya very much,
Fedya is happy
the feeling is mutual, he names
him Sharik (Ball), and Sharik
vows to guard the house, they all live
together, they don't need
nobody
but each other, when Matroskin
first met Fedya, he showed him that
a salami sandwich tastes better
when you eat it upside down,
so that the salami touches your tongue,
this became a Soviet inside joke, Lyosha
taught Pasha how to eat a salami sandwich
like Matroskin, and Pasha never ate
them any other way after that,
Lyosha loved Pasha
and Pasha loved Lyosha,
they weren't halves, but real
blood brothers to each other,
once they also found
a stray kitten in a bush on the edge of Maxim Gorky park
(though this one did not talk), it still had its baby fur,
messy light-grey down like a mad scientist,

with teardrop-blue eyes, Pasha picked up the kitten
and they took it home on the bus,
their mama (Pasha's biological mama),
took pity on the kitten and the boys who kept pressing
the small sticky thing against their cheeks, she put some
chicken meat that she softened between her fingers
on a saucer and put out a teacup of water, the kitten
slurped and chewed with narrowed eyes,
licking his mouth every gulp,
their papa came home late, he was called in
on a Saturday and was not
as tickled
by the sight of the kitten,
Please, Papa, Pasha begged,
Come on, Papa, Lyosha joined in,
but a No from a father
in the Soviet Union
was a No that would outlive
a fossil on the shore of the Black Sea,
they took the kitten back to the park
the next day, it was a Sunday,
to put him back where they found him,
Pasha cried into the folds
of Lyosha's windbreaker
on the bus, he tried
not to make too much noise,
he couldn't stop
crying, his mama said, Pashenka,
the kitten will find another home,
but Pasha knew about indoors
and outdoors, and even at six he believed
you only get one chance,
He will die, Pasha murmured, passing his tongue over the corners
of his salty mouth,
his mama lowered her eyes,

Lyosha told his little brother that time
passes and takes with it
everything, including
kittens and tears, Where do

they go? Pasha asked,
Lyosha kneeled down and cupped Pasha's shoulders,
Home,
Lyosha said,

but Lyosha
did not come home, he was a giant
to Pasha, but too young
to be talking like
a seer, he was teenage and teenagers shouldn't have faith
in the world that was left to them, Pasha
certainly didn't when he turned thirteen,
already American-versed, he had dropped his accent
right quick,
that same year he spent a night on a bench
in Lincoln park, curled up
with the chestnut fuzz of his new buzz cut
growing in, knees into his chest, one hand holding on to
his black-green jacket lying over his torso,
torn at the waist, it was a faulty
plan, he would devise better, he would
get the hang of running away, know what
to take and what to leave behind,
know who to answer back to and who to walk away from,
know how to walk past cops and how to look at the elderly
for some spare cash, you had to spot a granny or old man
who had that squint, you could tell their own grandkids
were giving them kick-back (American kids did that sort of thing,
they didn't have our Soviet generational discipline),
Pasha saw they just needed
a kid to look at them as if their lives
were in the old hands that've seen
how to care and how to scorn, they were stingy
but they gave a little something, it was enough,
that's what Pasha learned, that anything could be
enough,
if you made it so,
when I met Pasha, we talked in our
well-versed American, super-slick,
no one would've guessed we stood in line

at our parents' hips
for some kilos of chicken, Pasha wasn't
Jewish and he wasn't a woman,
but I had Jews and women who knew my plight, that's not where
we saw each other, Pasha knew who he was so deeply
that it made him completely
lost, like me, we fell and kept
falling, we couldn't live otherwise, at the end of high school
Pasha had changed his tune, he got
really academic, decided he wanted
to go to college and be a big shot,
he had always been smart, very, very
smart, he might have had some neurological gifts,
he never looked into it, but he had this crazy memory,
he could memorise a whole book, I'm not kidding,
he had a library in his head, and that's why
he remembered every poem he had come across,
he got a monster scholarship
for having a needle-point mind and for having been a political
    asylum kid,
that's how he ended up in Paris at a biotech lab, they were
developing gene therapies
to treat inherited forms of blindness, he had ended up specialising
    in rare
non-life-threatening diseases, he had initially been put on a long-
    term project
studying Leber Hereditary Optic Neuropathy, or LHON, he said I
    could just call it
LHON, but I really wanted to memorise the full name (the extent
    of my gift),
to sound a bit smart like him, but also to be part
of him, it's a highly uncommon mitochondrial disease
that induces irreversible loss of vision, there was also
a project on one with a name
I forgot, Retinitis something, it's where
the retina cells break down
over time and you go
blind, when Pasha came to Berlin,
he was on long-term sick leave, he said he was burnt out,
it was apparently common in his profession,

I had only known one other person
on long-term sick leave, he was also
brilliant and also worked in the medical research field, he had
Asperger's and schizophrenia, some people get dealt
a real hard hand, that's all I could think, and still
felt awful to reduce him to his playing cards,
we only talked for one evening, at a party, he was off his meds
for schizophrenia, because they made him sleep twenty hours a day,
and the upside was that without them he didn't need much sleep
    at all,
which was great for him, 'cause, God,
he loved life, he had obsessions, it had been foliage
for a while, and then it became cunnilingus,
he read every book – I mean every single book – ever published
on the topic, and I believed him, he wanted
to understand everything about
eating a woman out, I was glad
to find him at this party
that I didn't want to go to in the first place,
I had dragged myself out in an attempt
to not be idle in the face of depression,
he was full of life, he talked
my ear off, and I was happy
to not have ears for an evening, he had never
attempted suicide, Why,
he asked, did you want to die? I like people
who get right to the point, my beloved neurodivergents,
I didn't want to die, I just didn't want to live,
I'm open to
alternatives, I joked,
he began to list off some, I told him
I was making a joke,
he paused and smiled, his smile
was an artwork
of years of practice, I could tell
he loved life,
he gave me tips
for mastering the art of cunnilingus,
he couldn't really hold down a job, he told me,
'cause with the meds he sleeps too much, without the meds

he has episodes, I said it must be
torture, he said, It is
my life,
I had never thought of life
as belonging to me,

my favorite poem
by Joseph Brodsky
is called 'The Blind Wander At Night',
it's about a night,
a dark night,
a milk-dark night in Saint Petersburg,
a blind man is crossing
an empty square, it's a dark world,
a milk-dark world of a blind eye,
the blind man is walking through darkness
in the dark, it's about feeling around
the stones of a wall, stones
that still hold voices, it's about the lives
being lived
behind the wall, it's about the wailing
of walls, it's about dying
in the darkness,
it's about living
by touch, it's about light and shadow,

Pasha met Nadya
through me and didn't trust her, he didn't say so
but I could tell, 'cause he wasn't himself around her, which was
exposed and extensive, around her
he was pensive and terse, so that Nadya didn't recognise
the person I'd talked so much about, He's a special person,
I told Nadya in the kitchen,
she nodded but didn't
make eye contact,
he was a special person, and that, in itself, is
an addiction, or a way of keeping a faraway star
in the nebula, a person like him
shines most
in the darkness,

Serhiy Zhadan
is one of Ukraine's contemporary It-writers,
poet, novelist, translator, activist
(though the writer of the twenty-second century is by default
this type of Renaissance man), his language
is suave, offhand and tempered, quick on its feet,
slang, poise, revolt, it's a special
experience, in his novel *Depeche Mode*
(not so much about the British new-wave band,
but post-Soviet Kharkiv, 1993 to be precise, and the old radios
in the old Kharkov homes now play
denim, eyeliner, tattooed music, namely
Depeche Mode, but this is a detail), at the centre,
a gang of young do-nothings are bumming around a broken city,
in a broken economy of a broken country, they've got a lot of ideas,
but no jobs, they're full of zeal
to make something of themselves,
but nothing grows in the wasteland, they turn
their skills to transporting booze contraband over the border,
and selling it for more, they chit-chat
about dreams of various political governance,
turns out everything's a little
shit, there's a lot of running around to get
nowhere, there's one line early on
that was Pasha's refrain, he said, God,
who writes a thing like this? Pasha trusted
hard science, but idolised writers, the line was from the narrator,
nineteen-year-old Zhadan himself, in the midst
of liquor breath, vomit, morning trains, pretending
to be sober, bloody nostrils and guys who got nothing
but a good fight to make the day worth its while,
the young narrator, who's been waxing tough up until now,
switches his tone and admits that he's just
looking for a little bit of hope in it all,
in the darkest hour of the darkest day
of a black-milk life,
just a sliver of light, nothing big, the type
that comes out
when you open the fridge at night,
the image stuck with me,

and when I sought out the desolation of hours
that occur while others sleep, notably Nadezhda
in the bedroom, I would pace
into the kitchen and open the fridge door
and close my eyes and feel the cold bluish light
coat my skin,

Zhadan stayed
in Kharkiv when Russia invaded, where he's still
writing and coordinating humanitarian relief, Pasha's dad
used to ask him if he was remembering things correctly,
Pasha would get off the phone with blood-shot eyes, his dad wanted
    to know
if Pasha's uncle, his dad's brother, really did
touch him that one summer
after Lyosha died, Papa
got sent to one kolkhoz and Mama
to another, and if that was why
Pasha was gay . . .
his parents had divorced a couple of years
later, and his dad returned to Kharkiv,
met some *tyotya* so-and-so who was looking to put up with a tight-
    lipped Casanova,
a nationalist with dollars in the bank never hurt,
in Kharkiv he got a good life going for him,
so Pasha couldn't figure out why the old man
kept calling, trying
to warm up to the son
he had left in the cold, he told Pasha
that he believed him, of course he believed him, he was just
checking, 'cause you know children
and their imagination, But maybe it's children
who get all the facts right, Pasha divulged,
as he threw his mobile phone on the couch and it bounced
on the cushion, but did not fall on the floor,
God,
we loved life
at an arm's length, and both Pasha and I
had long arms, Nadyenka had
beautiful hands and chubby biceps,

144

I loved them, her hands and her biceps,
Nadezhda Nikolaevna and Pavlo Oleksandrovych,

not my Pasha, but another,
Pavlo Romanovych Lee,
Ukrainian mama and Koryo-saram (ethnic Korean Soviets)
    papa,
the thirty-four-year-old actor and TV presenter enlisted
on the first day of the Russian invasion, ten days
later, a muggy March,
he was hit by Russian shelling in Irpin
and twelve days later
buried in Vorokhta, where his mama
is amongst the living, the shelling
burst the same day I broke
one of Nadya's glass coffee mugs
(she loves glass and steel, anything
that is transparent or reflects),
she had told me I don't clean the apartment enough, so I was
cleaning the apartment enough, she had a particular way
of washing the dishes, couldn't stand
water droplets on the metal frame of the sink, I often
forgot to wipe them, I'm trying, I told her, she said
she knows, she can't help her reaction, but she knows, I know
she knows and can't help her reaction,
but what am I supposed to do with an eagle
glare upon the face of my beloved,
yelling at me with her mother's voice,
I was rushing to clean it up, and she was enunciating
her Russian at me, *Ostav*,
just leave it, *Ostav*, that she'd do it, *Ostav*, I took a step
in her direction only because
the broom was that way,
I shrieked, she shrieked,
and we both hopped around the glass pieces
to the couch, where Nadya pulled
out the piece of glass
from my heel, I told you,
she whispered with a mellowed tone,
to stay where you were,

back when
Nadezhda was unknown to me and known
to her ex-wife, she had broken
a blown-glass ashtray, it was so precious to Nadya,
and she broke it herself
on purpose, that's as far as she went
into the story, I gathered she had started breaking
the things most precious to her
on purpose, before someone else could, Nadya smoked
rarely, but loved it, despite
her asthma, she smoked the thin
Vogues, very Russian, her wife smoked
weed, a lot of it, it stank up the house, she'd buy
a loaf of sliced white bread and a jar
of Nutella and smoke up and scoop out
the spread onto the cottony squares and leave
the smudged knife to stick
on the glass countertop of the low table in front of the couch,
I never understood how Nadezhda put
up with such a woman, being a clean freak and
lovable, she said what brings people
together, keeps them together, I didn't
understand, did she mean destiny? (I assumed, because
the bedrock of her life choices seemed to be made on
one word), her joy
was destiny and her suffering
was destiny, destiny
was a jack of all trades, I guess,
I didn't believe in destiny at all,
nothing
is meant to be,
Nadyenka
told me I make her head hurt, please, she'd had
a long day, but Pasha and I could out-talk
destiny herself and still
have the stamina for another round
of devil's advocate, Pasha got interested
in eyes 'cause they are the most complex organ,
after the brain, and it's terribly beautiful,
that part of this organ sits

exposed to the world, our whole lives, though technically
we see with our brain, our eyes only let in
light, it becomes data
elsewhere, Pasha told me he would never forget
the stretch of lid and row of lashes upon each eye
on the face of Lyosha
in his casket, he remembers asking his mother why
his eyes were closed, because they were open
when he died, We need to close
our eyes so we can rest, his mother
explained,
the blind
can still see their dreams
(if they were not born blind),
Pasha stood by
the claim that the dead
continue to dream,
we both had an immense appetite
for abstraction, we took time
to define 'the dead', what does that even include,
the organic body, brain activity, or the soul?
what is dead when it is dead?
for someone who worked
for what can be proven, Pasha had
an incredible stretch of conception
for all that cannot be proven, it was
an antique faith, when science had room
for God, and God had room
for heretics,
like the Russian writer Yevgeny Zamyatin declared
in an essay from a collection titled *A Soviet Heretic*,
the world
would cease to be
without heretics,
Pasha talked and I listened,
I talked and Pasha listened,
we were both
free,
what is a dreamer
when there is no brainstem to be activated,

no limbic system to be stimulated,
what is a dreamer, when there is no more
future to be had, where do
those animals of an ancient language go
to roam? if you ask a farmer,
they'd say a pasture outlives
its animals,
does an empty
world still dream?
The dreams the dead have,
Pasha said, are a different sort,
Tarkovsky suggested
that we not hold dreams
to any other logic
than their own,
in the West
you know who to avoid
at a party, if they mention Tarkovsky,
but for us Easterners
it might as well be
Disney, no big head about it,
I always said Tarkovsky knows
how to bore a human to death,
boredom and death being
the main elements of Slavic craft,
I will never forget
lying in bed sheets I had long-promised myself
to wash,
streaming *Solaris*, one of his legacy films,
on a pirate Russian site,
crying
my eyes out,
needing
to live one more night
without eyes,
a thick coat of saline on the outside
of my nostrils, my eyeballs really felt
like they could just slip out
and fall
into my hands,

I cried
not for anecdote, but for the quiet
that eludes both God and science,
and for the soreness of a story
that is not your own,

Solaris is a distant alien planet
covered with an oceanic gel, discovered by a group of scientists
who believe it to be a living thing that can be
communicated with, Solaris
is a planet that reads minds
and generates delusions
in the form of those we have lost, I won't
spoil it, it's not about
a good mind-fuck, or a philosophical gimmick,
it's about being bored to death, and then
dreaming
the way the dead
can dream,
an iris has
256 unique, identifying characteristics,
whereas our finger only has
forty, That's why security uses
retina scanning more and more, Pasha inserted,
a reason to wear
sunglasses at protests,
there was a study that showed
that just the image of an eye,
a graphic, drawing, whatever,
motivates people
to exhibit behaviour
deemed morally appropriate, it's called
'the watching-eye effect',
I found a photo
in our sock drawer,
stuck in the crevice between the wooden panels
at the back, it was Nadezhda
and her ex-wife, they were both smiling
as if they had just had sex, their cheeks
roughed from the cold, behind them

a long Moscow boulevard lined
with threads of white sky,
I could see in Nadya's gaze
that she was happy,
I couldn't see anything
in her ex-wife's eyes
because they were
scratched out
with a black ballpoint pen,

Cupid
shoots an arrow,
because love is a wound,
that's the one thing
Nadezhda and Pasha
agreed on,

there's a saying
in Yiddish,
and it goes like this:
*di pen shist erger fun a fayl,*
the pen stings more than the arrow,
Nadezhda
signs her name with a slash through the letters,
crossing out
what she's just written,
it's how she signed
her name on her wedding certificate,
on my thigh with a blue pen when I asked her what tattoo I should
    get next,

and on those documents
from the police,

when we finished dancing and the bottle of champagne,
she held me by the waist
and told me that she wants to marry me,
not now,
but later,
she will marry me, I knew

she was drunk, and so was I, I knew
we both wanted something big
to happen, my love was betting
on the future, I let my eyes
slide and become blurry,
we couldn't make eye contact anyway,
we were swaying, it was making me
a little nauseous,

Dostoevsky was an awful gambler,
an addict, he pawned his wedding ring, he described it
as a fever, it all sounds very
literary, things that hurt the most sound very
literary, Nadezhda
was constantly sick
after she met me, she says she's always sick
when she's in a relationship, and perfectly healthy
when she's single, at the start
of our romance she got a thrombus
in her vein after a clumsy nurse's needle
in a routine physical
(if the clot had gotten into her lungs,
she could have died, Nadezhda often
reminds me),
two new polyps in her uterus
that needed to be removed
(a curse
from her mama's side of the family),
an abscess between her big and second toe on her left foot
(hard evidence that the world
was not on her side),
and a spinal inflammation
(figures, she threw her hands down
and let them wobble at her pelvis),
but Nadya was also tenacious,
she wouldn't let any
microbe get the best of her,
I'm what Nadya describes as
'an intellectual', my sickness
is just the existence of my own mind,

we lay
in bed, I was smelling
her hair, it smells like chamomile
when she sweats, I asked her
what she was thinking, she said
nothing, that her mind was completely
empty,
I have seen great sights,
Olympic cliffs, colossal waterfalls, snowy mountain crests,
I've seen an injured bird
take its last breath
and die on the cement,
I've seen
my own death
many times,
but I've never been able to even imagine
what it's like
to have an empty mind,
It's very nice, Nadyenka told me,
her jaw was soft,
all I could think about
was what it's like to think about
nothing,
I'd rather not know
these things and smell
the chamomile on the oily hairs
of her hairline,

Olha Kobylianska, one of Ukraine's leading writers of the late-
    nineteenth,
early-twentieth century,
and a little, kind of,
gay, was well known for her 1898 novella
called *Valse Mélancolique* (very à la mode
to mix French into Russian in those days),
about three young trail-blazing intellectual
women, friends pushing the limits
of roles to which they were subjected
in turn-of-the-century Russia, they are close
friends, very

close friends, it's the passionate
friendships that always gives
closeted authors away, though Kobylianska
wasn't hiding it either, the work
predated Virginia Woolf's *A Room of One's Own*
by thirty years,

Nadezdha has two
whips, one leather flogger, a tightly-woven
handle and thick stands of leather like a horse tail,
and a riding crop whip, a long handle with a small rubber paddle
at the end, the flogger gave a longer-lasting
sting, but the crop had that crisp snap and artistic
precision, we kept both by the bed, I liked
to be flogged once or twice, just to pull
my pants down and get a quick one-two,
we didn't even fuck,
I imagined Nadya was
a high lieutenant,
a woman on top
who hated women,
especially Jewish women,
it was too easy
to send them to the camps,
she always
set one aside and
taught her a lesson,
the lesson being prolific and biological,
it would take
many sessions
to explain,
and it needed
to be explained
with tough
love,

the notion of destiny or fate
is a little different
in the East, there are three words
that are untranslatable,

*sud'ba* (something like fate),
*dusha* (something like soul),
and *toska* (something like depression),

*sud'ba* is less airy, it does not come
from above
the curtains of the clouds,
it is the weight
in our feet
when we stand
and the weight in our chest
when we lay,
it is more organic and less
ordained, it comes from the verb *sudit*,
meaning to judge,
*dusha* is the soul, but it's also more
than the soul, it is also the spirit and the pulse,
it's also freedom
and emptiness, it is room
for more,
it is the ability to hold
that which is gone
and that which we await,
it comes from the verb *dishat*,
to breathe,
*toska* is a longing,
and a memory and a dream,
it's grief,
and homesickness
for things and people we've known
and things and people
we haven't yet encountered,
I guess it's closest
to the Portuguese word *saudade*,
nostalgia for that
which we do not know,
or the Greek *nostos algos*, a physical
pull or ache for time gone by,
*toska* comes from
the verb *taskat*, to drag something heavy

around, *toska* makes us gloomy, solitary,
and wise, there is a way
of getting wisdom through
grieving, and in the East, you don't need
tragedy to grieve, you can just grieve
life itself,


one
of Anton Chekhov's early
works is a lesser-known short story called
'A Little Joke',
and it goes like this:
it's a bright winter afternoon, a city gentlemen comes to a small
        town
where a young and pure-hearted woman,
Nadezhda Petrovna, lives,
the gentleman, who's the narrator of the story,
is stuck in this small snowed-in village, so why not
enjoy what is to be enjoyed,
he tries to convince
Nadezhda to go sledding down the mountain
with him, why not
enjoy the company
of a young and pure-hearted
woman? Nadezhda Petrovna
is terrified
of that mountain, he coaxes her,
he's got a charming way
of putting the pressure on, she agrees,
they climb to the top
of the white hill,
he seats her behind him
on the sled, takes her arms
and wraps them
around his waist,
they speed down the packed snow,
the icy wind
rasping their cheeks,
mid-air
the gentleman whispers,

*Nadyaaa Naddddyyyyyaaa,*
*Ya lyublyu tebya,*

the wind rushes
his words behind him
past Nadezhda's ears,

he's not sure
why he said I love you to this girl, but why not,
you can't take life
too seriously,
they scrape to a halt and Nadezhda
is in a stupor,
she tells him she never wants to go down that hill
again, she nearly died, her heart
is beating faster than a rabbit's, in that rush
of blood are the words,

*Nadyaaa Naddddyyyyyaaa,*
*Ya lyublyu tebya,*

did the city gentleman
really proclaim them,
or was it just
the wind playing tricks on her?

Nadezhda studies
his face, his cheeks
are rosy, his beard holds flecks of snow,
she can't tell,
was it him
or the wind?
suddenly she's imaging a life
in Saint Petersburg
with him,
she would be
a city gentlewoman
she had never daydreamed
of this

before,
the gentleman comes back
the next day,
she's terrified
of that hill,
but she says yes,

they whizz
through the sunny chill and mid-air
the gentleman whispers,

*Nadyaaa Naddddyyyyyaaa,*
*Ya lyublyu tebya,*

for the hell of it, why not
enjoy a refrain?
the sled slows and comes to a halt
at the bottom, Nadezhda is breathless,
she squints at the gentleman's
eyes, posture, gait,
she can't tell,
she can't sleep
there is a whole life
out on that hill,

the next day she asks
the gentleman to go sledding, he's not
got much going on, he's happy to entertain,
up they go,
from the snowbank on the hill,
Nadezhda holds on
tightly to the gentleman,
he kicks them off to a start
with his boots,
the snow sprays from the blades
up to their faces, mid-air
the gentleman whispers,

*Nadyaaa Naddddyyyyyaaa,*
*Ya lyublyu tebya,*

there's something quite beautiful
about a motif, why not
keep on saying it?

his beard, the whisper, the ice,
Nadezhda has a fever
at night,
and one desire
in the morning:
to go
sledding,

the pair
continue like this, day after day, Nadezhda,
sleep-thinned and tormented, the descent
that throws the two clinging bodies
mid-air,
between earth and sky,

*Nadyaaa Naddddyyyyyaaa,*
*Ya lyublyu tebya,*

winter fades,
the snow melts,
soil and green-brown grass poke through,
it's time
for the gentleman to head back to Saint Petersburg, his trunks packed,
his carriage ready, Nadezhda stands by the window, watching the
     horseman
coming down the street, she holds her breath, maybe
he will stop
in front of her house and knock
on her door, and tell her
finally to her face,

*Nadyaaa Naddddyyyyyaaa,*
*Ya lyublyu tebya,*

she sees
the profile of the gentleman

in the window of the carriage, he
does not turn to see
her, the horseman is far now, spring
is here, years later

the gentleman comes back to visit
that little town, he stops by
Nadezhda's house, she's still
there,
he peeks through the window,
he sees kids, a husband, and a grey
tired face belonging to Nadezhda,
he pinches his brow,
remembering the packed snow,
the sharp winds,
that frozen hill,
and the arms of a young and pure-hearted woman
holding his waist
for dear life,
he purses his lips in deep
thought, he still can't quite
remember why
he said those words, it must have been
a joke,
a little joke,

there's a Yiddish saying,
and it goes like this:
*Az men vil nit alt vern,*
*zol men zikh yungerheyt oyfhengen,*
If you don't want to grow old,
hang yourself while you're young,

the last years of Nadezhda's relationship
with her ex-wife
were made up
of threats to leave
on both sides, though both sides
were not equal,
Nadezhda was a permanent resident in Germany,

her ex-wife only a legal resident through a marriage
wherein she was a financial obligation
to Nadya, Nadya paid
all the bills for both of them, took on an extra job
selling cosmetics at the Galeries Lafayette on Friedrichstraße
on the weekends
for both of them, she said she had never felt
so humiliated
in her whole life, standing behind
the glass counter, knowing the woman
she married
was smoking weed
on the couch, I asked her why
her ex-wife didn't pay her share, Nadya said
I loved her, and that
was the answer that
scared me to death,
I brought her, Nadya told me,
to Germany, I did all
the paperwork, I found us an apartment,
I got her covered under my insurance,
I used up
10,000 euros
it was my whole savings, she
sweet-talked and did graphic design
side-jobs, she had
money, I didn't ask for it,
she didn't give it,
all Nadezhda had, in her eyes,
to loom above her ex-wife's head,
was a police report, a simple police report,
which would boot-kick
the woman she had been sure
was the love of her life
back to Russia,

She fucked on the side, Nadya added,
I saw messages
on her computer, I was asking the same question

I had been asking Nadya since we met,
I didn't want
to blame Nadya, I just wanted
to understand, I added before
and after the question, which I guess was a sign
that I did blame her,
after a certain time span
of this, it was up to her
to leave, and I was tired
of hearing the story, I had used up
my compassion, I suppose
Nadya became a Greek daughter
doomed to tell her story
till the end of time,
come back to earth, Nadyenka,
without your veil,

but then I started paying attention
to the gaps in the story, I started to look
at her life in two dimensions instead of three,
the layers flattened and the lapses
filled in, between the fights
were the gleaming white sneakers
her aunt had given her, on her wedding finger
wound the breath of her father's stout liquor,
and when Nadya tore the envelope
to read the police report,
I was already resting my nose on her hairline
smelling tiny white daisies
boiled and strained,

together with Nadyenka
we were home,
we had a roof
and an origin,
I already
left Ukraine,
I can't
leave Nadya,

my therapist
did not give her blessing
to my way of thought,

do the shipwrecked
tangle their limbs together
because they are in love,
or because they don't want to be taken away
by the water?
*Ya lyubyu tebya,*
*Nadyezhda,*

Nadezhda stood in the entryway
of her building
on Ilsestraße
and tore the edge
of the envelope
towards her,
then pulled out the folded
documents
and unfolded
them,

she said, Can you believe that
you can live
for years and years
and die
in just five seconds?
that's how long
it took her
to unfold
the stapled
papers,
she doesn't even remember
if she got the keys out of her purse
or if they were already in her hand,
she was standing
in front of her open mailbox
and then she was leaning
on the kitchen table

signing
her name,

You're not stable,
Nadya told me in a raised voice, you need my help,
I told her yes,
I do not have
the stability of others,
but I am stable,
I know I'm stable,
that's why I see a therapist once a week,
and why I'm taking my medication,
and why I have spent the last ten years
learning about compassion,
I had told her
my diagnosis, it has a reputation
for being a bit scary,
I know first-hand, it scares
the shit of me, so I can imagine
it falls into the red
zone, but I'm trying, I told Nadya,
and it shows, I've made it
this far and I can regulate
myself, she made me sit down
and explain the disorder
at length, it wasn't
the most humiliating thing I've gone through,
but close,
the internet
made it worse,
I didn't choose
to be this way, now
I was crying, not because I was ashamed
of having what I have, but of having
to justify
my sanity
and human competency,
I have worked
very hard, I don't do all that
shit to myself anymore,

do you know what it's like
to stop, Pasha knows what it's like
to stop,
most people are born,
and they take living for granted,
but there are those who have to choose
to live
over and over again,
even Nadya's breathing
was loud, Okay, she said,
All right,
not seven days
after this talk she looked me in the eyes
and said, You're a mess,
but I won't stop
loving you,

my family stopped
going to Israel
'cause everyone we went there for
had died,
Vova had taken us
in his four-door white Mazda
into the valley,
next to the army training base,
three times
and we had washed
the three tombstones and put
three plastic bouquets at the feet of their graves,
Vova died
too, he was getting to that age,
I'm not sure
if he passed before
or after his birthday, Vova's son
had moved to Canada I heard,
Toronto, he and his wife
grabbed their chance, a paediatrician and a nurse practitioner
are always needed,
especially in the last handful
of years, their son died

on the Lebanese border, they couldn't sell
the four-door white Mazda, by that time
it was all huffs and puffs, they just left it
at the junkyard, I don't know
who drives the old folks in Ibicur now,
into the valley,
next to the army training base,
to wash the tombstones and leave
plastic flowers at the feet of the graves, I think
Vova's son's son was into techno music,
he had gone to a festival
in Hamburg
on one of his times off
from training, I got this email
in Russian
from a Levi Rubinsky, saying something about
his dad's dad driving
my mama's mama
to her mama's grave, he got my email through the grapevine,
he was travelling around Europe,
mentioned some music festivals,
I didn't know any of them,
festivals give me anxiety, plus
I think my heart's too weak for that kind of lifestyle,
he had some time off, maybe Paris,
I gave him my mobile, told him, Don't hesitate,
apparently he did hesitate,
never heard from him,
got word that he died, I assumed
it was during a military operation,
but who knows, he could have
been on his way to the grocery store
to buy a bag of Bissli chips
and a couple of persimmons,
and tripped over a rock,
and hit his head on the curb,
while an Israeli street cat,
with that deformed
alien face, vertical
eyes, and tufts of hair

missing, approached
and licked
the pool of blood, God
is consistent,

there's a Russian techno song called
'Plachu na tekhno' (Tears at the Techno)
by Cream Soda (collab with Khleb),
a Moscow-based electro house
group that started in 2012, they're anything but
serious, that early '90s zest and synth-pop groove, they made
the song in 2020, in the middle of quarantine,
and their video
with eclectic dancing on balconies
went viral, brought the disco to the stoop,
but the song is full of
sorrow, a dreamy synth beat
with a voice that is alone,
a girl or maybe a boy,
or a boy who wants to be a girl,
or a girl who's afraid of her country's
womanhood, she's come to the disco,
he's come to the disco,
she's looking for the one
who's in her heart, he's looking,
he said, she said, they would be there,
but they are not there,
the Euro-techno is rising from the synths,
she is not alone,
he is not alone,
the club is full,
it's a rave, it's dark,
but she knows
the one in her heart
is not there,
his heart knows
darkness
that is not shared,
the flashing lights
stream all around

it's dark in his heart,
it was once
so bright, she's looking,
he's waiting,
so many bodies,
but they are not
that body, in 2012
a Moscow gay club called 7Freedays was raided,
glass bottles in the air, tables falling to the floor,
fists and knees, boots
to the gut, October,
red earlobes and bloody noses, the club
was celebrating
International Coming Out Day, thirty
complaints were filed, no one
was arrested,

the dance floor is spotted, fluorescent glimmers,
in the dark, she is waiting,
he is standing still, the one in his heart
is not there,

100 people
broke into the attic of Central Station, the biggest gay club in
    Moscow,
disabled the wiring, stole the sound system,
that month
in 2013 there were twenty attacks,
armed men protecting
Russia
from paedophiles,

it's dark in her heart,
it was once
so bright, she's looking
for the one who said
they would come,

Solyanka, Nadezhda's Solyanka, 2014,
Mikki Blanco was set to play, it was the middle of the night,

it was dark outside, and dark inside,
the way we like it,
the group pushed their way through the doors,
it's easy to push your way in
when you have weapons,
they were protecting
Russia
against the perverts of Solyanka,
they shut off the electricity,
it's a different type
of darkness,

the techno is getting good
in the song, Cream Soda knows
how to mix it so that
you've just got to
dance,

*Dance, Dance,*
*Cry, Cry,*

now the singer, the girl or the boy,
the one who is alone
on the dance floor,
has eyes full of tears,
and the tears cling to their lashes
and let go,
and there are
tears at the techno,

*Roskomnadzor*
is Russia's state-run media watchdog,
common complaints are
porno, minors, brothels,
illegal drug use, it's enough
to raid a rave,

the two women who own the Saint Pete lesbian club Infinity,
took a flight in
from Moscow

where they happened to be seated
a row in front of
Vitaly Milonov,
the most powerful Russian anti-LGBT politician,
they snapped a quick selfie
of them kissing
with Milonov in the background,
the shot went viral,
Infinity
was raided
shortly after,

the dance floor is packed, she is standing
still, he is standing
still, it's hard
to dance when the one who's in your heart
is not there, and you're
crying
at the rave,
droplets pulse
with the techno base,

two clubs, 2017,
in Minsk, Burlesque and Casta Diva,
stormed, the dance floors were packed,
the bodies were
detained,
passports were
demanded,
copies were made
and filed,

Rabitza Club in Moscow,
muscle against the one
who's in someone's
heart, shiny cheeks, shiners,
the music was good, until –
it's hard
to dance
with your arms pinned behind your back,

the synth beat is so dreamy,
the hips want to ebb and the shoulders
want to veer away
from the body
into the darkness,
because the voice is alone,
and it belongs to a girl,
or maybe a boy, a boy
who wants to be the music,
or a girl who's afraid of her country,
she's lovesick
for the one who is in her heart,
but not in the club,
it's hard
to dance
when you don't know
if the one in your heart
is dead or alive,

Potemkin club, 2019, in Dnipro, Ukraine,
two dozen police officers,
some armed, some masked,
broke down the doors,
everyone was just dancing, and then
nobody was moving,
the music cut off,
the cops pointed
their guns around, the barrels at eye-level,
it was dark and everybody was dancing,
and now, it's dark and everybody is down on the ground,
the cops opened all the windows, it was five
degrees outside, a good night
to have a quick smoke and
exchange numbers,
everyone was dancing, and now
they are lying belly to the cold floor,
the cops are telling them not to move,
they are making their rounds,
it's hard to dance
when there are guns

in the air, everybody
was dancing, now they are lying
belly-first on the icy floor,
for three hours,
it's hard to dance
when your limbs
are going blue,
they say it was a different time, parents
buried their children, their weird
children, I'm trying
my hardest so that my mama
doesn't have to bury me,
it was a different time when
you could play guitar
on a whole nation's ribs, it
was a different time,
the boy
stabbed his brother
for fear that he might
love him
the way that he is, it was
another
time, they say,

there's a song,
that's more just speaking
over drowsy piano keys,
it's the dark-milk voice of Mikael Tariverdiev, an Armenian
from a different time, that of the Soviet Republic of Georgia,
it was written by Grigori Pojenian, born, like me, in Kharkiv
from a different time, that of the Soviet Republic of Ukraine,
he was half Armenian, half Jewish, he sailed
the Black Sea with the Soviet marines, he wrote
poetry, he wrote this song called 'I am a tree', he is
a tree, Tariverdiev exhales in the song, the piano chord releases,
others want him to be like an evergreen, bright in the snow,
they want him to be like a willow, malleable by touch,
but, Tariverdiev exhales, he is a different
tree,
the piano chord releases,

they want to use his bark, a tree can be
peeled, sawed, dried, all of the parts can be used
to make
a mast of a ship or a red violin, but,
Tariverdiev exhales,
he is a different tree, the piano chord
releases, he wants
to reach for the sky, perhaps to pull himself
out of the soil and
walk, perhaps to write
a poem on his own
skin, we
are different trees, they
talk about roots,
deep roots furrowing deeper
into the earth, we don't want to go deeper
into the earth, we are
weird but
alive, we want to look
out our small window and count
the leaves,
the crows,
our meds,

Nadyenka is on Ilsestraße, fifth floor,
leaning against the kitchen table,
signing the documents
she's just received,
she closes her eyes
and there is the prowling stare
of her ex-wife
across the dance floor,
Solyanka
is the place to be,

on Ilsestraße, fifth floor,
there are papers waiting
on the kitchen table,

when time is unfolded
and flattened open,

Nadyenka and I are carrying
groceries past the Kurdish kids, she's telling me
a story,
I'm not listening,
I'm too sleepy,
being sleepy
is better than being anxious, I told my psychiatrist, that's why
I continued with those pills, despite their
side effects, Nadya stops
saying what she is saying,
I struggle
to keep my eyes open,
but when I do, I can see across
1324 kilometres,
to a snow-white Saint Pete,
where a blind man
is crossing the square,
he leaves
no footprints,

Nadezhda signed her name,
and shortly after, her ex-wife
was notified
that she is no longer
legally eligible
to stay in the Federal Republic of Germany,
boot-kick, love
is a wound, love
is paperwork,

I had to do it, Nadyenka told me,
Why should she
live the life
in Berlin
that I paid for
with my sanity?

Nadyenka tells me she loves me
more than she has ever loved
anyone, I tell Nadyenka

that I love her
more than I've ever loved anyone,
our lease is sitting
on the kitchen table
under a big clouded stone
we brought back from Spain,
the wind blows
from the passing train of the Neukölln U-Bahn station a couple of
    streets down,
from the wide-open field that was once the Tempelhof airport,
from the end of one winter
to the beginning of another,

we are here on Ilsestraße, fifth floor,
in our bedroom
sitting knee to knee,

I'm in my double-XL men's black sweater,
she's in the black jeans that pinch her belly,
I don't look good in necklaces,
but I'm wearing the one
Nadezhda says I look good in,
the sterling silver one
with the heart,
she hasn't changed out of her work clothes,
I've been wearing the same clothes I've been wearing
all day, I haven't left the house,
she's just come home, we both just want
a home,

it is dark here on Ilsestraße, fifth floor, on the darkest
hour of the darkest
day of a Berlin black-milk winter, and we have chosen
not to turn on the light,

her palms lay open
in her lap,
my palms lay closed
in my lap,

yesterdays and tomorrows,
the wind blows,

in the darkness,
there are three words
between our bodies
*sud'ba,*
*dusha,*
*toska,*

I miss my brothers,
I miss the verses
of the dead,
I miss a country
that has no time,
I miss my home,
even if
it had no territory,
I miss my head,
even if
it got unscrewed,
I miss my childhood,
even if
it made me lose my mind,
I miss Pasha, God,
I miss Pasha,
he missed
the darkness
he had glimpsed
when he was ten years old,
he missed Lyosha,
and Lyosha missed
his adulthood,
I miss the first thread of blood
that comes out of a cut
I will never again make,

the first time Nadya and I
had sex

I opened a bottle of red
I had bought with great care
to impress, we drank
half a glass each, and left the rest
to sour, we couldn't wait
to get naked
with each other,
I had been sad,
so sad
before I had met Nadezhda,
and then I was happy,
so happy,
and horny,
and a little nauseous
(my meds don't mix well with red wine
for some reason),
but I was too horny
and happy to give over
to seasickness,
we took off
our own clothes
with functionality,
there was no time
for stylistic stripping,
I wanted Nadya to lay
her flesh
upon my flesh
so desperately
it felt like waiting
at the hospital,
Nadya laid
her flesh
upon my flesh,
we crammed our tongues
inside each other's mouths,
we nicked teeth,
strands of her hair pasted with saliva
clung to my chin,
she rode my hip bone

and pressed her knee
between my legs,
her thigh was all wet
from me, my hip was all wet
from her, my eyes were closed
because it was dark
anyway,
she had turned off the lamp
somewhere in our haste,
I opened my eyes
and Nadezhda was the body
on top of me,
pushing into me,
above me,
it was dark
with the lamp off,
I couldn't see much,
the edges of things,
her ears, her shoulders, the top
of her head
were faint against the dimness,
there were no contours,
no outlines
to separate her body
from the room,
the room
from the world,
our lives
from the past,
I was looking for
her face,
and it was hard to make out
that it was her face,
it was dark,
but there were
two eyes
that flashed
on the precipice
of the roof,

I was coming as she finished
coming, our voices overlapped
like a Gregorian chant,
and then it was quiet,

my eyes were very hot,
and they overflowed,
the tears ran down my temples,
Nadya rolled next to me,
I turned into her,
burying
my forehead
against her collarbone,
I didn't want her to see me crying,
but I wanted her to feel me
crying, I hadn't cried like that
in a long time, who knows,
maybe that's how I cried
when I was born,
I wasn't embarrassed,
but I mumbled, I'm sorry,
because we didn't know each other yet,
even though
we've known each other
for the last four billion years,
do you remember, Nadyenka?
you squeezed me into your whole body
and I felt so contained, we were both
free,
I thought you understood why
I was sobbing like that, why
I was pressing myself as thin as paper
against you,
it was nothing,
it was nothing at all,
it was nothingness,
it was the darkest day
in all of history,

there's a joke
and it goes like this:

a CIA agent is sent on a mission to Moscow
to assess the state of the new Russian Federation
under Boris Yeltsin,
following the economic and political collapse
of the Soviet Union,
the American carries in the pocket of his trench coat
a dark green leather notebook
wherein he gathers all the necessary information,
he visits a grocery store, the shelves
are depleted,
he writes
in his dark green leather notebook:
*There is no food,*
then he goes around the clothing shops,
the racks and stands
are deserted,
he writes
in his dark green leather notebook:
*There are no shoes,*
he steps out and begins to walk
to the bank, when a Russian man grabs him by the arm,
What do you think you're doing? the man huffs,
I'm just writing, the American replies,
Writing, eh? the Russian repeats,
Yeah, just writing, the American nods,
the Russian looks over both shoulders and then back at the American,
You're lucky, he says,
that we are now free,
ten years ago, you would have been
shot
for that,
the American shakes off his ruffled sleeves
and opens his dark green leather notebook,
he writes:
*There are no bullets.*


Nadyenka, my Nadyenka,
my beloved Nadezhda,

the dead are dreaming
of us,
they are drinking
black milk
they got from a platoon
who don't know
why
they are following
a furry grey kitten
across the ice,
I'm trying,
I'm stuttering the words
*Ya lyublyu—*
to the translator
so the translator
can tell the journalist,
so the journalist
can write it down,
God,
I love Nadezhda, and, God,
I love life.

# Acknowledgements

Thank you
to my mom, who is always my first reader,
to my dad, for making me my favourites: blueberry pancakes,
  borscht, squeezed cabbage salad,

to my therapist,

to those who transformed me with their love,

to the Snowapple Residency in Mexico, Jackie, Chow, where I
  wrote the last passages of this novel,

to Jane, my agent and guardian angel,

to Candida and Vidisha and everyone at Footnote, Vicki, Rose,
  Dhruti, Grace, I don't sleep lightly and I don't take dreams
  lightly, and you are a dream come true of a publishing team,

to my silly, childish hope for peace,

and to Anoushka,
my cat.

# About the author

**Yelena Moskovich** was born in Kharkiv, Ukraine (USSR) in 1984. She is the author of three novels: *Virtuoso*; *The Natashas* (both Serpent's Tail) and *A Door Behind A Door* (Influx Press) which was longlisted for the Dylan Thomas Prize. She emigrated to the US with her family as Jewish refugees in 1991, then again on her own to Paris in 2007.